Jack Vance

Nightlamp: an Outline

NIGHTLAMP:

an Outline

Published by Spatterlight

Cover art by Howard Kistler

ISBN 978-1-61947-351-5

Amstelveen,
The Netherlands

www.jackvance.com

Jack Vance

Nightlamp: an Outline

Foreword

How does a writer get started? After an idea pops into his mind, what is the process that leads to a finished story? At one extreme there is the writer who starts with a single draft and counts on his editors to help it to its final form. At the other end of the spectrum is the writer who proceeds through many drafts, adding, subtracting and revising until he is satisfied with the result.

Jack Vance was closer to the second extreme. He began with what he called an outline, which was in fact a telling of salient elements of the story, realized in varying degrees of detail, which was then fleshed out with nuances of characterization and additional incidents. Typically these outlines would be read by a prospective publisher and form the basis of an assignment to complete the narrative, accompanied by an advance against royalties.

Most of Vance's outlines are lost. Two saw print before the advent of the Vance Integral Edition, three more appeared in the VIE's addenda volume. All of these have appeared in volume 62 of the Spatterlight Press Signature Series.

"The Kragen", effectively an outline for the novel *The Blue World*, appeared as a stand-alone novella in the July 1964 issue of *Fantastic Stories of Imagination*; it was also anthologized in *Mythical Beasties*, edited by Isaac Asimov, Martin H. Greenberg, and Charles G. Waugh (New York: Signet 1986).

The Genesee Slough Murders, intended to be the third Joe Bain mystery, was printed in *The Work of Jack Vance: an Annotated Bibliography & Guide* by Jerry Hewett and Daryl F. Mallett (Penn Valley, CA, and Lancaster, PA: Underwood-Miller 1994). In this case, the publisher declined to continue the series. Robert Ockene, Vance's editor at

i

Bobbs–Merrill and an enthusiastic supporter of his work, died, and his successor proved to be less receptive.

Appearing only in the VIE and subsequently in the Spatterlight Press Signature Series, in addition to screenplay proposals and revisions of earlier publications, are outlines for three unrealized works:

1. "The STARK", a proposal for a series of stories about a generation starship;

2. An untitled mystery which the VIE called by its first line, *The Telephone was Ringing in the Dark*;

3. *Wild Thyme and Violets*, inadequately described as a Gothic novel.

Among the many fascinating documents now in the possession of the Vance estate are outlines for four of his last completed works. By this time, his vision had deteriorated to the point where he was no longer able to compose in longhand; rather, as he himself once noted, he had made the leap from the pen to the computer without the intermediate stop at the typewriter. Thus these texts are preserved entirely as computer printouts, with an exception in the case of *Ports of Call* to be adumbrated at the appropriate point.

The present volume features *Nightlamp*, which of course became *Night Lamp*, Vance's last stand-alone novel (or, if you prefer to think of *Ports of Call* and *Lurulu* as a single story, his penultimate work of fiction). Of the works previously mentioned, it is most comparable to "The Kragen", being a fully-realized story, requiring only a final revision to clean up such details as sociology and character names, unnecessary repetition and infelicitously-formed sentences. Thirty years earlier, it is quite possible that that is exactly what Vance would have done, but by the mid-nineties he was no longer writing for the pulps.

Instead, he proceeded to fill out this nearly 60,000-word narration, which is comparable in length to his masterpieces of the sixties and seventies, more than doubling its length. The differences between the two, *Nightlamp* and *Night Lamp*, offer insights into Vance's creative process, not only the title itself, but the many decisions made along the way. It is strongly recommended that, if you haven't already read

Night Lamp in its final form, you drop this volume on the spot and proceed to do so.

Probably the first difference that a reader will notice is the change of the names of the protagonist's step-parents from Luel and Perseia to Hilyer and Althea. Why? The question cannot be answered, perhaps not even if Vance were here to tell us. For more than half a century readers marvelled at the fecundity of his imagination, not least in his ability to find exactly the right name for a character, city, planet, institution or religious sect. His computer hard drives contain numerous files whose contents consist entirely of proper names, the vast majority never used. Here, selected at random, are a very few:

Spingola Spanglehammer

Swanghammer Sulfornio Duse

Dangwirtle Peeble

Osro Madel Doy Farlock

Ryncey Clois Garlock

Gossum Pannic Slade Gossaer

Plaisance Quantic

Other names are works in progress as well. Is Dean Hutsenreiter's given name Clarens or Paulinus? Never mind, it will be Clois when all is said and done. What of the Black Angels of Penitence, who attack Jaro to punish his 'schmeltzing' and are themselves punished in turn? In the first place, their own name for their little band is still in flux at this point: they are Angels of Death, Angels of Vengeance, Angels of Merciful Death. And the lads themselves morph from Hanfer Irmerankin, Aubry Cudd, Jehame Wistenor and Kocson Herdy to Hanafer Glackenshaw, Kosh Diffenbocker, Almer Culp and Lonas Fanchetto. The vancean font of appellations is evidently bottomless, and however felicitous a name, especially for a villain, may seem, there is always a better one just waiting to be fished out.

Even heroes are moving targets. The man who will turn out to be Jaro's father, Tawn Maihac, is originally Dain. When he introduces himself to Luel and Perseia, he uses the name Evan Tarr, but when he introduces himself to Hilyer and Althea, it is as Gaing Neitzbeck. Both of these worthies were Maihac's shipmate, but Tarr has not survived to the present day. Neitzbeck, however, is necessary to the expanded story, as it is he, rather than Tarr/Maihac who will instruct Jaro in the arts of combat, much to the dismay of the Angels.

The original Evan Tarr is not present, because he fell in the fighting that resulted in Garlet's apparent death and Maihac's capture by the Loklor (or rather Loclor). And on which world did this take place? Where is the fabulous Romarth? Why, on the planet Maz. Terry Dowling, who read and commented on this outline, noted that Vance had used that name in *The Dogtown Tourist Agency*. So Maz becomes Fader, a name also previously used in the story "Fader's Waft", which makes up the bulk of *Rhialto the Marvellous*. This is of course, as Patrick Dusoulier has pointed out, only one instance among many of name recycling in the vancean oeuvre.

A few names do survive the process: Forby Mildoon, Lyssel Bynnoc, Thanet, Clam Muffins, Gallingale, Asrubal — and of course Jaro Fath and Skirlet Hutsenreiter.

Still, as entertaining as these details may be, they are less significant than matters of plot and milieu that required multiple iterations to achieve a final form. Here, Jaro is not freed of Garlet's voice in his brain until he frees Garlet from Asrubal's dungeon; perhaps because the voice was a serious obstacle to the developing relationship between Jaro and Skirlet, it had to go. Making a virtue of necessity, Vance introduced the Doctors Windle, Gissing and Fiorio, who "isolated Ogg's Plaque from its sheathing of nervous impulses", thus silencing the voice. In the process, they provide a generous share of comic relief.

Many of the most important characters are already drawn in something like their final form. Jaro, Maihac, the Faths, Garlet, Asrubal: though there are differences in detail where their individual experience is concerned, they are largely the same people in both versions. The striking exception is Skirlet Hutsenreiter, or Skirl as she later prefers to be called — though the change in preference is motivated differently, and is the particular consequence of something she acquires in *Night Lamp*: a story of her own. Her experience on Marmone in Chapter 10 is a new invention that, much more than her father's impoverishment and death and the loss of her home, provides a motivation missing from *Nightlamp* for her resolution to become an effectuator. It confers on her an individuality that invites comparison with the finest of vancean females: Jean Parlier, Luellen Enright, Madouc, Wayness Tamm, Betty Haverhill. This development also has a parallel in the progression from "The Kragen" to *The Blue World*, which is enriched by the introduction of Meril Rohan.

Vance's novels are, among many other things, characterized by a plethora of stagnant, stultified societies which his protagonists proceed to turn upside down. The guilds of Ambroy on Halma, the Chilites of Shant on Durdane, the Chaschmen of Dadiche on Tschai: these are only a few examples. Nor is Romarth spared. But in *Night Lamp* Vance takes pity on the Roum and at least provides them with a path to a less catastrophic future. In *Nightlamp* Jaro, Maihac and Skirl simply turn tail and run, leaving the Roum to stew in their own juices.

The most far reaching evolution, and the most difficult to describe, is the realization of Thanet itself, with its hierarchy of clubs and endless striving "up the ladder". All the elements are here, but not until the final version will inconsistencies be ironed out and the workings of comporture elucidated, yielding a vancean society as finely chiselled — and as hilariously absurd — as any he created.

And of course there is the ending and the ultimate fate of the Jaro-Skirl relationship. Suffice it to say that *Nightlamp* treads the path later to be taken in *Ports of Call*, while *Night Lamp* echoes the resolution of the Glawen-Wayness liaison in *The Cadwal Chronicles*. Both approaches seem plausible, the latter perhaps requiring its more finely drawn Skirl to work. A brief scene between Skirl and Maihac in Section 2 of Chapter 15 ingeniously tells us all we need to know:

> "Does Jaro know you are talking to me like this?"
>
> "Definitely not! Jaro is perhaps just a bit vain. He would never suspect that you might prefer wealth, comfort and safety to dying some unspeakable death in his company."
>
> Both Skirl and Maihac laughed and parted friends, and the subject never arose again.

The text presented in this volume is identical to that of the computer printout from which it is taken, save only for the correction of obvious typing errors. No attempt has been made to correct inconsistencies in names or plot. It is highly probable that, had Jack Vance taken the steps necessary to ready this text for publication, he would have made more changes than that. Rather than anticipate the process that ultimately resulted in *Night Lamp*, Spatterlight Press offers this text as Vance left it, before turning an eminently readable story into a masterpiece.

— *Steve Sherman*

Chapter 1

1.

Jaro's earliest recollections were glimpses and impressions: blurred images of structures, faces, vehicles, landscapes: none coherent with any of the others. Two of these, or perhaps three, were especially vivid. All were heavy with emotion. The first, possibly the earliest, induced a sad-sweet ache which brought tears to his eyes, even during his later youth and adolescence. He seemed to be looking over a beautiful garden, silver and black in the light of two pale moons. Sometimes there was an instant of displacement, as if Jaro might be someone else. But how could this be? It was himself, Jaro, who stood by the low marble balustrade looking over the moonlit garden, out to the tall dark trees along the face of the forest beyond.

There was nothing more to the recollection; it was brief and dreamlike, but it afflicted Jaro with longing for something, or somewhere, forever lost. As time passed Jaro tried to avoid the thought and push it to the back of his mind, especially when a sad muffled voice, speaking words he could not understand, began to be associated with the image.

Other early recollections affected him with far different emotions. One of these, the glimpse of a man's silhouette in the twilight, caused him a pang of terror he could not control, even when the time for such a fear had long passed. The man stood at no great distance from the house where Jaro and his mother lived: a tall ominous shape against the blue-gray sky of dusk. He wore a low-crowned hat with a stiff brim; a frock coat of severe cut, which emphasized long arms and a spare torso. He stood with legs apart, brooding across the landscape. In Jaro's recollection, he turned his head to stare at Jaro, eyes like four-pointed stars gleaming with silver light from the otherwise blank face.

There were other recollections, not so sad nor so frightening. Jaro remembered a yellow clapboard house close by a copse of tall segmented grasses or reeds, with the river flowing nearby, and in the back yard the tumbled ruin of a concrete shed which had become his playhouse. These images were ambiguous. Sometimes he sensed the presence of his mother, though he could not see her face. Then, in the blink of an eye, the mood could change; the silhouetted man might appear, and after that: sheer terror. On occasion his mother spoke to him, and he heard her words with clarity. They were always the same: "Never must you falter; never submit! Do as you must do! Now I will die, without fear, since my death gives you life. Oh my poor Jaro! To think what I must do to you!"

And then, sometimes —wonder of wonders! —Jaro seemed to hear another voice sounding from deep within his mind. It said: "Have no regret! I am brave, I am true! I can endure."

This was not his mother's voice. It came from a part of his mind that was not altogether under control.

There were other recollections: cold water, darkness, drifting, total misery which was more of a mood than a recollection; then, for a time a moil of unclassified confusion: struggle, pain, a yelling time which was half-oblivion, and which he never fully remembered.

2.

Luel and Perceia Fath, savants of good reputation, occupied chairs of middle prestige at Thanet Institute on Gallingale. Both sat in the College of Philosophy, where their fields of study complemented each other; Luel analyzed systems of aesthetic symbology; Perceia studied the music of barbaric or semi-barbaric peoples, typically performed on unique instruments, using unconventional scales to produce bizarre harmonies. Such musics were sometimes simple, sometimes complex, usually incomprehensible to alien ears, though often fascinating. The two areas of study dove-tailed so neatly that the Faths were able to plan joint research expeditions. One of these trips took them to the world Hamil's Fancy and out upon the Kadafarene Plain, east of the Wyching Hills. Their base was the village Stronk, where they hired a vehicle, intending to visit a camp of Kadafarene Gypsies, fifty miles out on the steppe.

As they drove their vehicle along a road at the back of the Wyching Hills, they came upon an unsettling scene. Four gangling peasant boys armed with cudgels were carefully clubbing to death a squirming creature which lay in the dirt at their feet. Despite oozing blood and broken bones, the creature tried to defend itself and fought back with a desperate gallantry which transcended bravery and seemed to the Faths sheer nobility of spirit.

Whatever the case, the Faths thrust the boys back from their limp victim, who they now saw to be a dark-haired urchin five or six years old, emaciated as if from hunger and dressed in rags.

The peasant boys stood resentfully to the side. The oldest explained that the creature was a wildling, no better than an animal, who would, if allowed, grow to become a robber or a depredator of crops. It was sensible to exterminate such vermin when the best opportunity offered, as of now, so — if the travellers would be good enough to step aside, they would get on with the job.

The Faths, though approaching middle age, and conditioned to a life wherein contradictions between abstruse philosophical concepts provided the most drama, were still energetic and decisive. They scolded the slack-jawed peasant lads, then with great care they lifted the battered child into their vehicle, while the peasant lads looked on in baffled disapproval. Later they would regale their parents with the weird conduct of the odd folk in funny clothes, who might even have been off-worlders, for the peculiar way in which they spoke the language.

The Faths took the injured child to a medical facility and were unreasonably cheered to find that he had suffered only broken bones and would soon be as good as new.

The Faths spoke to the boy during his convalescence. They noted, pedantically, that his verbal skills were excellent though his accent was strange to them, and quite unclassifiable. He could not recall his name, but thought it might be long and complicated.

"What of your parents: where are they?"

"My mother was killed by the tall man with the starry eyes. My father went away, and my mother said that he is dead."

He closed his eyes and seemed to rest, his thin face almost lost in the softness of pillow. With his eyes still closed he said weakly: "Garlet? No; that is not my name." He winced and seemed to struggle, then opened his eyes. "I am Jaro. That is my name."

"Who is Garlet?"

Jaro sighed and closed his eyes. The nurse came forward. "He is emotionally exhausted. He needs to rest."

Perseia reached down and took Jaro's clenched fist. She stroked it and the fingers slowly relaxed. "You are safe now," said Perseia. "Rest and sleep, and don't grieve."

Jaro, still with his eyes closed, spoke in a sad soft voice, almost too quiet to be heard: "But why must I be locked in the dark?"

Perseia said: "You are not locked in the dark, Jaro! And you never shall be! Do not fear such things!"

Jaro, half-asleep, paid no heed. He was resting easily and the Faths departed.

Jaro awoke and lay staring up toward the ceiling. The nurse brought him nourishment and spoke to him, but Jaro was still unable to remember his past existence.

The Faths made inquiries at nearby towns, but discovered no reports of missing children, and the authorities at the hospital told them that children were abandoned as a matter of course in the Wyching Hills; Jaro's case was not exceptional. The episodes of disassociation which they had noticed were probably hallucinations stimulated by shock, terror and deprivation. Jaro doubtless would pull together the remnants of his memory in due course. In the meantime, the boy seemed alert, self-possessed, and even intelligent. All in all, his prognosis was good, and he seemed to have suffered no permanent impairment of any sort, other than a trifling confusion of memory and an odd reference to disembodied voices.

The Faths were childless. When they came to visit Jaro, he greeted them with obvious pleasure which tugged at their heartstrings. He was clearly something more than a few rags and bones of human flotsam. When the Faths returned to Thanet on Gallingale, Jaro accompanied them. Presently he was legally adopted, and began to use the name Jaro Fath.

3.

The Faths lived on a fifty-acre farmstead off of Gwendolyne Road, two miles north of Thanet, in a ramshackle old three-story house named 'Merrihew' — in its original meaning a supernatural creature of delicate beauty something like a fairy, with gauzy hair and webs between its fingers. If one captured a merrihew and nipped one of its ears, the merrihew became bonded to the person who had done the nipping, and must serve as his slave forever; Jaro was assured as to the validity of the legend by the Faths, and saw no reason to disbelieve so pleasant a possibility, and whenever he went walking in the forest or along the meadow he moved silently and stayed on the alert.

The house Merrihew was built of weather-stained timber, with an eccentric roof of many gables covered with ageless ironstone tile. The original farm had encompassed two hundred acres of meadow, a pair of forested knolls, a small river. The Faths had sold two flat fields at the west of the property to a truck farmer, but had kept fifty acres along with the knolls and the adjoining forest, a segment of the river and a pair of meadows laced with stony outcrops.

Jaro was assigned living quarters at the top of the high-ceilinged old house. His early troubles faded from memory. Luel and Perseia were affectionate and tolerant: the best of parents. Jaro, in his turn, brought them only pride and fulfilment; before long they could not imagine life without him. Their only concern was that he seemed overly self-contained. He was soft-spoken, when he troubled to speak at all. At school he made few friends and avoided group activities, including games, and was therefore considered a 'loner' — not a term of approbation on Thanet, where social skills were held in high esteem. The schoolwork itself gave Jaro no trouble; his teachers considered him almost on a par with the notorious Skirlet Hutsenreiter, whose intellectual prowess was the talk of the school, as was her haughty and imperious mannerisms. Skirlet was a year or two younger than Jaro: a slender erect little creature so strongly charged with intelligence and vitality that, in the words of the school nurse, she 'gave off little blue sparks in the dark'.

Skirlet was of moderate stature, slim but not thin; boyish, though clearly a girl. She was far from ill-favored, with short thick dark hair clasping her face, which included thin flat cheeks, a stern little nose and a wide mercurial mouth. Eyes of a particularly luminous gray looked from under fine black eyebrows. Despite what might be considered adequate reason, she seemed to lack personal vanity, and she dressed so simply that her instructors sometimes wondered as to the solicitude of her parents — all the more surprising, since her father was the Honorable Clarens Hutsenreiter, Dean of the College of Philology, and a 'Clam Muffin', at the most rarefied level of Thanet social hierarchy, far surpassing even the Squared Circles.

Jaro first became aware of Skirlet when she was jumped a grade and placed into his own class. It immediately became evident that Jaro had an intuitive grasp of mathematics quicker and easier than that of Skirlet, and for the first time she found herself in a secondary position. It was almost as serious as an intimation of mortality, this sudden revelation that other superb minds existed, presumably controlling mental universes as complex as her own. Had Jaro been odd, or misshapen or a bizarre genius, she would have accepted the situation with equanimity, but Jaro was quite normal, obviously clean, nice looking, if aloof, pensive and even more indifferent to her than she to him.

Skirlet at last accepted the situation philosophically. She was far too proud to be graceless. She was after all a Hutsenreiter, whose patrician training allowed her to express whole volumes of meaning by the loft of an eyebrow or the twitch of a lip. No question; it was a fine thing to be born a Hutsenreiter and a Clam Muffin! Things were the way they were. Unfair? Not necessarily. If you had something good, you might as well enjoy it; if not, it was wasted.

Jaro, for his part, was barely aware of the girl with the square shoulders, the short thick dark hair and the buoyant uninhibited conduct. He knew that she was reputedly clever; he rather admired her taut little body and the swagger with which she conducted her affairs; otherwise she was a face among many. At this time Jaro had no great interest in girls and, more urgently, he was preoccupied with other matters. These were causing him an increasing uneasiness.

The facts relating to Jaro's early life had never emerged, and as time passed they became of ever less concern to the Faths.

For Jaro, however, a peculiar condition not only persisted but had taken on a slow sullen new strength. This was a voice speaking just under the level of intelligibility at the back of his mind. Occasionally, Jaro seemed to catch an isolated word or even a phrase; the balance of the remarks were carried away as if on the wind. The mood of the voice was plaintive and seemed to tell of grief and loss. Jaro tried to ignore the voice and pushed it as far back into his mind as possible. Sometimes the voice subsided into the remote perspectives of a landscape, only to swing about and come careening back like the figure on a carousel. When Jaro heeded the voice, he became disturbed. One day on impulse he confided his problem to the Faths, who instantly took him to the clinic for psychiatric evaluation.

With as good grace as he could muster, Jaro discussed his problems with the psychiatrists. He mentioned that sometimes, most often while dreaming he felt himself plunging through the dark upper atmosphere, naked, free, wild, propelled by nothing but the force of will. The psychiatrists gently assured him that these flights were sheerly dream sequences, probably instigated by the pressure of a full bladder. Jaro frowned dubiously. Plunging naked through the night-time sky, with stars overhead? An insistent bladder? There seemed no continuity of ideas. Perhaps the psychiatrists saw deeper into situations of this sort than the untrained layman. It was no great matter, since in any event he could not control his destination, and wandered through the dark like a lost soul. More important, said Jaro, was the voice which spoke at the back of his mind. The psychiatrists gave him their full attention. What, they asked, was the purport of the communication? Jaro said that he could never quite grasp the import of the words; they were always just beyond the edge of intelligibility, though the mood of the voice was evident. There was a clear burden of grief and loneliness and inexpressible longing.

The psychiatrists attempted hypnosis, but encountered a barrier which caused them perplexity. "He is not in active resistance," they assured the Faths. "Still, we feel some sort of barrier closing off his mind, as if he were already under subliminal commands."

Another of the psychiatrists added portentously: "Not impossibly those he has imposed upon himself."

The first psychiatrist said: "It is also possible that we are dealing with a multiple personality."

"Strange!" mused Luel Fath. "Very strange indeed."

Perseia shook her head. "I can't really believe it. Jaro, of all people, is sane and strong; he has proved it."

"We shall try again," said the psychiatrists. "This time we will increase his susceptibility with a dose of laxin."

Jaro was finally induced to talk under hypnosis. His voice rose and fell, and at times took on a different timbre, and the psychiatrists glanced sidelong at Perseia in something like triumph, as if to say: "You see? We were right all along!"

The significance of what Jaro said was never clear. At times he used the voice of Jaro Fath; at other times he spoke with the emotion of someone isolated and lost in a place from which there was no escape. Jaro associated this feeling with his recollection of the moonlit garden — though there seemed no rational connection. The voice sometimes rose in quavering clarity, like a tendril of smoke: "So goes my precious life, ebbing away in the dark. Oh how can it be? Why must it be?"

The psychiatrist asked: "What is your name?"

"In the dark there is no need for a name." The words were barely audible, and there was no further response to questions: only the singing stillness of solitude and black void. Then Jaro spoke, in a clear voice: "I will talk no more." His eyes closed and he slept.

The psychiatrists explained that Jaro clearly had been a victim of infantile trauma; that his subconscious mind had decided that the early events were too terrible to contemplate, and had scrambled them into a collage of shapes, colors and stray quirks of emotion. The resulting farrago could no longer affect the conscious perception and hence was less dangerous than brute facts. Still, no one could guess what damage such a roil of fear, pain and hate could work upon the mind.

"So — what is the correct therapy?" the Faths wanted to know.

"Time," stated one of the savants. "It is the great healer."

Another expert proposed a more active therapy, which in effect mapped out the brain, codified the networks, disassociated everything, then carefully restored order, reestablishing broken links and interruptions, much as an organizational program reorders the disassociated clusters and fragments in a computer's memory. The process, however, was several orders of magnitude more complex, nor was it without adventurous possibilities for the mind so reorganized. The technique was not wholly under the control of the operator. If all went well, the patient would arise from the couch a whole person, his memory intact and all his capabilities functional, even though he seemed less spontaneous, more docile and agreeable than before. On the other hand, the fluctuation in the spin of ten electrons, or the intrusion of a few unwanted phosphorus atoms and the previous condition might he exacerbated, which of course was regrettable. This particular therapy, so the Faths decided, was too extreme for Jaro's rather mild symptoms. The psychiatrists warned that there might be a sudden degeneration of Jaro's apparently healthy condition, and stated that they were willing to risk the procedure. The Faths still would not agree. The psychiatrists suggested other methods of treatment. If the circumstances of Jaro's past were made known to him, in all their intimate and evocative detail, the knowledge might well exorcise Jaro's private demon, who grieved so pitifully at the back of his brain. The Faths said, Yes, that seemed reasonable, though the program would entail a great deal of research over who knows what vast distances of space, at large expense. The psychiatrists agreed that this would seem to be the case. The Faths said that they would think the matter over and departed.

The psychiatrists retired to their refectory for their afternoon tea. One of them commented upon Jaro's somber self-possession. "I had the uncanny feeling he was watching us more carefully than we were watching him."

His colleagues laughed uneasily. "Nonsense," said another of the team. "You are suffering from a guilt neurosis!"

"True enough, but is this not the seminal force which impels us all?"

"Allow me to pour you some more tea," said one of his colleagues, and the topic was put aside.

Jaro assured the Faths that he was cured of his problems and there were no more psychiatric evaluations, to the relief of everyone.

The next day at school Jaro was sitting on a concrete bench outside the school library, looking through a book. He turned his head to find Skirlet Hutsenreiter sitting at the far end of the bench. She sat sidewise, one leg tucked up under the other. She was watching him with concentrated interest, so that her fine black brows formed a straight line across her forehead. Skirlet was careless in regard to clothes; today she wore pale gray trousers and a dark gray shirt with a white collar.

Jaro courteously acknowledged her presence. "Hello."

"Hello," said Skirlet.

Jaro returned to his book. After a moment Skirlet spoke. "I am curious. You are Jaro Fath?"

"Correct. And you?"

Skirlet raised her eyebrows. "Surely you know that I am Skirlet Hutsenreiter."

" 'Skirlet' is an unusual name. I should have remembered you on that account alone."

Skirlet, taken aback, said distantly: "It is short for 'Shkirzaksian' which is my mother's country estate on Marmaude."

"Interesting." Jaro returned to his book, but Skirlet again distracted him. "You also are an interesting case. That is why I am here. Do you mind my watching you?"

"It all depends," said Jaro. "How closely do you intend to watch and for how long?"

"Not too long, and certainly no more closely than is absolutely necessary."

"I suppose it will be all right then."

Skirlet held out her hand, touched her thumb to each of her fingers in turn. "Can you do that?"

"Yes, I should think so."

"Show me."

Jaro performed the feat. "How was that?"

"Quite good. Do it again... Again... Again."

"That is enough for now," said Jaro. "I don't want to start myself on a nervous habit."

Skirlet clicked her tongue in vexation. "Tsk! You've broken the sequence. Now we'll have to start all over."

"Not unless I know why."

Skirlet made an impatient gesture. "It is a clinical test. Deranged people start making characteristic mistakes at specific counts. I heard that yesterday you had been declared, well, just a bit crazy by the psychiatrists, and I wanted to try the experiment as soon as possible."

"While I was still crazy after dealing with the psychiatrists, you mean."

"Not exactly. I wanted to study your basic derangement."

Jaro struggled for words. "At least I now understand your attention. At first I thought that you had fallen in love with me."

"Oh no," said Skirlet without emphasis. "I have no interest in that sort of thing. In fact, I don't even like you very much."

Jaro sat looking at her, wondering what went on behind the composed thin-cheeked little face. As he watched, Skirlet plucked a blade of grass and began to chew on it, as insolently as possible. Jaro abandoned logic. "Why is that?"

Skirlet considered. "You are far too vain — that is part of the reason. When I come into the room you don't seem to notice."

"Not true. If nothing else, you are unusual, and extraordinarily intelligent — not in my class, of course. You are even pretty in a perverse sort of way. It's clear that your mother doesn't dress you to Clam Muffin standards."

Skirlet spoke with dignity: "I dress to suit myself. My mother is on Marmaude, and she is not coming back. Here she is only a Clam Muffin. On Marmaude she is a Grandee of the Purple Radiance, and lives at Castle Cladesby."

"Is that good?"

"It's good enough to keep her away from Gallingale and my father who spends all his money on foolishness." Skirlet gave a sour chuckle. "There was foolishness at the castle too. I was required to walk around the garden naked every morning at dawn, and it was sometimes very brisk. But no one cared so long as there were nymphs running through the garden. Ah well." Skirlet sighed. "I'm none the worse for it, and I have become a connoisseur of foolishness. Now then: shall we go back to the test?"

"Absolutely not," said Jaro. "It won't work unless you have a crazy person to work with. I am not that person."

"You are not crazy?"

"I'd be the first to know."

"What of the psychiatrists?"

"I don't know whether they are crazy or not."

"What I mean is: why did they say you were crazy?"

Jaro shrugged. "I told them about something mysterious. They could find no explanation, and in the end filed my case in the 'C' docket."

" 'C'?"

"For 'crazy'."

Skirlet twisted her mouth into an expression of doubt. "Surely that's not true."

Jaro smiled. "I think they said I was 'off the chart', or something of the sort. Someone mentioned a 'one-armed accordion player', but I don't think he meant me. In any case, they could not solve the mystery."

"What is this mystery?"

"It is too complicated to talk about."

Skirlet was not pleased by the tone of the remark. She rose to her feet and marched away with head and shoulders rigid. Jaro sighed. Once a Clam Muffin, always a Clam Muffin. By extension, once a Skirlet Hutsenreiter, always a Skirlet Hutsenreiter. He returned to his book.

4.

At the start of the next school term Skirlet Hutsenreiter was not on hand, and it was learned that her father, Dean Paulinus Hutsenreiter had placed her in an exclusive private school, where she would receive an education appropriate to her station in life.*

Time passed. Jaro was graduated into the Lyceum, where he would be prepared either for the Institute or a career in the non-academic world. Jaro became a young man strong and spare of physique, somewhat taller than average, with square shoulders, narrow flanks. His features were almost classically regular, with a hint of austerity.

---

* The system of status gradation peculiar to Gallingale, while arbitrary, occasionally irrational or even mischievous, was nevertheless firmly based upon public acceptance. In theory the law recognized no social distinctions. As elsewhere across the Gaean Reach, the original doctrine had become so encrusted with layers of usage, custom, and special circumstance as to be unrecognizable.

At different times, under different circumstances, a hundred different adjectives were used to describe Jaro: 'sardonic', 'vain', 'moody', 'intricate', 'brooding', 'arrogant', 'reckless', 'patrician', 'solitary'. Jaro occasionally learned of these opinions; he was more amused than otherwise. Perhaps some of the terms had relevance, he thought, but none of them seemed to define his natural disposition. During periods of introspection, he sought for his own words to characterize himself; always he was distracted by the surge of sad inner sounds. Jaro decided that, if nothing else, he was 'patient'. Sooner or later the truth about his beginnings must surface — but when? There was no way of knowing.

Jaro had no taste for games or other group activities: a trait which was regarded with suspicion, as probably a sign of secret vanity. Such opinions could not be avoided; on Gallingale a remorseless scrutiny revealed everyone's exact status, in every category — financial, moral, intellectual, 'schaionie'*, and made any attempt to put on airs useless, even ridiculous.

One of Jaro's instructors reported to Perseia: "Jaro is always alert and fully alive, but he gives the impression that his thoughts are straying far afield."

"Oh! I am sorry to hear this," said Perseia, though she knew the trait very well. "I will suggest that he —"

The instructor held up his hand. "Please don't! Jaro does his work with an almost contemptuous facility. I have no real cause to complain,

---

* Untranslatable; an idea unique to Gallingale. Roughly, a person's dignified though restrained willingness to accept advancement in status without actually seeming to strive for it — like an ability to blow hot, cold, north, south, east and west at the same time. 'Schaionie' was a most subtle nicety of conduct mixing ambition, dissimulation, humility, stoicism, artful manipulation of circumstances in a single component which the folk of Gallingale understood very well yet would find impossible to define. In short: everyone longed for augmentation of status and worked to this end, though they strove to disguise the yearning. The medium which connected and lubricated the concept was 'schaionie'.

It may here be noted that the impulse was present, though somewhat attenuated in the psyches of Luel and Perseia Fath, but absent in the case of Jaro, whose ambitions never included permanent residence on Gallingale.

though this is what makes his day-dreaming so vexing. He is, for a fact, unfailingly polite and at the same time the most baffling of persons; can you understand him?"

"No," said Perseia with a sigh. "I am no more aware of what goes on in Jaro's mind than you."

To the gentle dismay of Luel and Perseia, Jaro showed no great interest either in music or the theory of aesthetics. They had hoped that he would follow them into the cloisters of academia but Jaro gave them no encouragement. When Luel or Perseia set themselves to discussing his future career, Jaro could only shake his head. "I can't decide on anything just yet. Nothing interests me enough that I want to specialize in it."

"Unfortunately," said Luel drily, "unless you do specialize and make yourself an expert in some field or another, you condemn yourself to a lifetime of low-status labor."

"I'm sure you're right," said Jaro. "I'll have to think seriously about the matter."

But when Jaro considered the future, he quickly found himself at a place where the possible tracks of the future branched into opposite directions. The voice at the back of his mind was preeminent. He knew the voice must be expunged before he lost the strength to cope with it. Over the years he had learned how to minimize the effect of the voice upon his mood. Often he could disregard it entirely, even when it chanted its anguish in the most poignant of terms. Sometimes it seemed to drain away into the darkness, quiet save for an occasional low gasp of grief, but if Jaro chose to listen, it was always there. Sometimes the emotion seemed to be directed against Jaro himself; at other times, when the emotion reached its wildest, most incoherent outbursts, it seemed as if the cosmos itself were at fault, or perhaps it was the simple concept of 'Being', naked and pure.

Jaro would resolve the mystery of the voice and release it from its torment, though how, he had only the glimmer of a scheme: he must systematically find the answers to a set of urgent questions. These included:

Who am I?
Where is the moonlit garden? How did I come to be lost?

Who was the gaunt man who stood so dark and ominous against the twilight sky, his eyes blazing like small fourpointed stars?

What harm had he already brought into Jaro's life?

When Jaro thought these thoughts, he felt an eery tingling of the skin. Someday the truth might be made known to him. He could not imagine living out his life in ignorance. But then: what of practicalities? To investigate required money. The Faths were moderately well-off and Jaro knew that they would give him whatever he asked for, no matter whether or not they approved of his purposes. Under these conditions he could not take their money.

5.

The Faths lived at Merrihew, a rambling old barn of a house, situated in a forty-acre meadow two miles south of Thanet. The countryside was pleasant; at the back of the property rose a forested hill from which flowed a little rill, which passed through the garden at the back of the house. To one side grew a dozen gnarled old fruit trees, which despite their age, dutifully supplied an amplitude of fruit each year. Merrihew, while run-down and in need of paint and minor repairs, was roomy and comfortable. Even so, Perseia and Luel occasionally considered putting the property up for sale. "It's peaceful out here now," Luel stated, "but I've heard talk that a land magnate wants to develop some of the land hereabouts into an enormous complex of houses and all kinds of facilities. If that ever happened, we'd be in the middle of worse clutter than if we lived in a small place next to the Institute."

"It probably won't happen," said Perseia. "Sufficient unto the day the evil thereof, and I like this tumble-down old house. I'd like it even more if you would fix the window and splash on some paint."

"I'm not gifted in these skills," said Luel. "Ten years ago I fell off a ladder and I was only on the second rung."

So Merrihew continued to function as before, without style or distinction, and nothing but airy space, light and comfort to commend it.

Jaro on occasion walked out into the forest and up the slopes of the knoll, where he had dammed the rivulet to create a little pond. One afternoon when he was sixteen, during the summer between his Fourth and Fifth term at the Lyceum — he was then sixteen years old — he sat beside the pond with his back to a tree, reading from an old book he had found in the shelves of the Faths' library. He heard steps, a sliding sound, and down the slope of the knoll, half sliding, half running, came a girl in blue trousers and a white shirt. She wore her dark hair carelessly short; Jaro saw that it was Skirlet Hutsenreiter. She was still slim and light-footed but could no longer be mistaken for a boy. Jaro rose to his feet; Skirlet saw him and stopped short. "What are you doing here?"

"Breathing, in general staying alive. What about you?"

Skirlet studied him a moment. "Your name is Jaro Fath."

Jaro nodded. "You are Skirlet Hutsenreiter."

The girl nodded. "Nowadays it is just 'Skirl'. I am minimizing, and discarding a great deal of useless paraphernalia."

"What are you doing with 'Hutsenreiter'?"

Skirl winced. "Nothing. My father refuses to change. I'm more or less obliged to use the name because it is so on legal instruments and things of that sort. A bit of a nuisance, of course. What have you got there? A book? Let me see." She took the book, glanced through the contents. "How to Tie One Thousand and One Knots." She studied a few of the illustrations, then glanced toward the tangle of cordage beside the side the tree where Jaro had been practicing a know of complicated knots. "What is that you are tying?"

"It would be a Turk's-head of eleven strands. They are interesting knots. Three-strand, four-strand and five-strand Turk's-heads are all tied differently, but once you know these basic weaves you can tie as many strands as you like."

"Hm. Can you tie these mat-like things?"

"If I take the time. But they are drudgery and not much fun."

Skirl returned the book. "It looks interesting, but I'm involved in glass at the moment, and I don't have time for anything else."

"'Glass' — how so?"

"I mix the ingredients — mainly sand and flux — I heat the mix in a retort, then I blow bottles, or cups, or goblets. At our house we use nothing else except the ware that I have made."

"Fancy that!" said Jaro. He looked her up and down. "I've heard somewhere that glass-blowing develops the chest."

"I don't know about that."

"You're not as flat-chested as you used to be, but I don't think we can blame it all on your glass-blowing."

"That is ridiculous," said Skirl. "You haven't changed much. I don't see a big beard or a mustache."

Jaro laughed. "Give me time. If the truth be known, you've become rather pretty."

"That is something I prefer not to discuss," said Skirl loftily.

"Oh? Why not?"

Skirl spoke with cool deliberation. "I've said enough. I don't want to create a role for myself in your erotic speculations."

"Just as you like," said Jaro. "If necessary, I will speculate about Lyssel Bynnoc."

Skirl raised her dark eyebrows. "Lyssel? She is a sly bag of tricks. Speculate away, to your heart's content. But first, what is in that packet?"

"Lunch. Cheese, apple tart, fruit. There is enough for us both."

"Naturally, I will pay for what I eat," said Skirl proudly. "Although, now that I think of it, I am not carrying any money today."

"I will feed you for free, as an act of charity."

Skirl had nothing to say and accepted Jaro's largesse without comment. He said, "You did not mention why you came here today."

Skirl pointed toward the north. "We own the land yonder, across the river. A man in town wants to buy it. My father as usual is short of funds, so I suppose he'll sell the land."

"Who is it that wants to buy?"

"His name is Forby Mildoon; he's in the real-estate business. I think he's a bit unscrupulous; besides he belongs to one of those vulgar Square Circles. I don't suppose you're a member?"

"I don't even belong to the Dog-catcher's League. I'll be leaving Gallingale as soon as I possibly can."

"Really?" Skirl was surprised. "You won't be going on to the Institute?"

"I hardly think so."

"Why not? Your grades are good. Next to me, you were the most intelligent student at the school."

Jaro nodded, smiling. "True! That is how I remember it!"

"Then why will you be leaving Thanet?"

Jaro looked off across the pond. "I'd almost like to tell you. But I'm afraid."

"Of what?"

"You couldn't possibly understand. You would listen, then go off and tell your friends of your adventure and the odd story you had heard."

Skirl shook her head. "Do you really take me for such a sneak?"

"No. But I find it hard to speak."

Skirl shrugged. "It's nothing to me, after all."

Jaro decided that he wanted to tell her. "You won't repeat what I tell you?"

"I promise I won't."

Jaro heaved a sigh. "First of all, the Faths are not my parents. I was born off-world. My mother was murdered when I was five; I barely remember her, and there is some kind of mystery involved. I think that we were fugitives. My first memory is a beautiful garden at the back of a marble palace, in the light of two moons; the memory haunts me."

Jaro paused. "There is even more mystery here: sad, tragic mystery."

Skirl sat frowning, hugging her knees: a pretty dark haired imp. "How do you know?"

"I can hear someone crying out in grief — right now, if I care to listen. It is something I don't understand. Either some part of me is caught somewhere and is suffering, or someone close to me is in pain. Or possibly I have something wrong with my brain: a freakish short circuit that keeps circulating a sad voice."

"What does the voice say?"

"It is always just beyond comprehension. It could be maddening, except I have trained myself to ignore it — but only temporarily. As soon as I can find enough money, I will go to find out what happened, and why."

"That is all very well," said Skirl, "but are you not a bit hasty? You should better complete the Lyceum, then take a degree at the Institute, so that you will have credentials to place yourself in a high-status career. That is what is most sensible, or so it seems to me."

"And to the Faths as well. But I don't want a career at the Institute."

"Then what will you do?"

"I intend to work in space. Perhaps I'll become a space vagabond*."

Skirl rose to her feet and stood looking down at Jaro with compressed lips. "Sometimes I would wonder about you," she said. "Now I think I know. You don't respect anyone — not the Faths, not Voirly Trase or my father or anyone else in the Clam Muffins, nor any of the faculty, nor even me! You have no reverence for the careful structure of our system and its basic nobility!"

Jaro rose to his feet. "Why are you angry with me?"

"I did not say I was angry."

"Anyway, I know why."

"Why then, if you are so perceptive?"

"There are two parts. First, I am startled by your intelligence, but I don't show enough respect, and I don't seem to notice your connection with the Clam Muffins. But I assure you that it's all a mistake; I am dumbfounded and I have noticed!"

"That is totally absurd!" said Skirl. "I am not at all vain. We both are aware of my intelligence; why bring the matter up? And as for my status, I am about to join a select group, the Quantarsi, from which Clam Muffins are barred, by reason of their overt elitism. So much for your first part; I am only amused. What is the other part?"

Jaro hesitated. "It's so secret I can only whisper it into your ear."

"Very well." Skirl tilted her head; Jaro bent toward her ear. Skirl cried out: "Ooh! You bit my ear! That's not what you were supposed to do."

"No," said Jaro. "You are right. I am abashed. It seemed a good idea at the time, but it was wrong. Let's try again."

Skirl looked at him skeptically. "I'm not sure that I trust you."

---

* The term here rendered as 'space vagabond' has no contemporary equivalent. It signifies a person who gains a livelihood — often precarious, often at the fringes of legality — as a space man, crewing aboard space ships or working at spaceports, without a fixed place of residence. The word has a thousand overtones, romantic, unfavorable, wistful, envious, scornful. Hereafter, the word 'vagabond' will be used in place of the cumbersome, if more precise, term 'space vagabond'.

"Of course you can! Your ear is safe. I won't blow, pant, or nip."

Skirl came to a decision. She shook her head. "It's quite absurd! You should be brave enough to tell me this secret to my face."

"I should be — but I'm not. I'll tell you some other time. Now, if you like, I'll drive you home."

"I prefer to walk."

"It's two miles, quite a long way."

Wordlessly Skirl accompanied him through the trees to Merrihew, where Jaro used Perseia's runabout to drive Skirl to her elegant home on Nardessus Hill, with the campus of the Institute spread out below.

6.

The Faths often entertained dinner guests, usually colleagues from the Institute. Toward the end of Jaro's second term at the Lyceum, Perseia brought home a rather unusual guest: a man of many competences and a background which had obviously included many events. His name was Evan Tarr. At the moment he lived nearby in the suburb of Ruthven, near the spaceport, where he was employed as a technician in the repair shop. Perseia met him as a result of her studies in the field of barbaric peoples' music; hearing of his collection of exotic musical instruments, which he had accumulated across years of wandering space, she was certain he could tell her much.

Evan Tarr's age was indeterminate but he was something past his first youth. His stature was average; he was lean, weathered to the color of old wood and seemed to be constructed of leather and steel wire. His face was bony, somewhat askew by reason of a broken nose, and a scar down his left cheek, which raised the corner of his mouth into a crook of sardonic humor. Another scar cut across his scalp, ruffling his coarse dark hair.

Evan Tarr's voice was gentle and his manner mild; and perhaps due to his luminous gray eyes, no one seemed to consider him ugly. His vocabulary was that of an educated man; however, he spoke little about himself or his past, save to intimate that for years he had owned and operated a small space freighter, which provided unscheduled service to remote and isolated ports-of-call. He had known many strange adventures, much fear and violence, which had earned him his scars and a desire to die in a comfortable bed.

Jaro, liking few people, was instantly drawn to Evan Tarr, who exemplified all of the attitudes and standards which Jaro had gradually been developing for himself.

Luel, however, was more skeptical, less fascinated by Tarr's presence. He considered Tarr a vagabond and declared that it was anyone's guess what sort of activities had kept Tarr busy off in the far wild corners of the Reach.

Jaro began to visit him at the spaceport, where he worked as a mechanic, trouble-shooter and demonstrator for the space-yacht agency. After a time Jaro began to turn to small jobs and make himself useful as best he could. Evan Tarr neither encouraged nor discouraged him, and Jaro cautiously widened his activities: cleaning, oiling, performing tough and dirty jobs, at the same time watching Tarr attentively and trying to learn without calling attention to himself. He worked with great care and diligence, trying to do each job perfectly. His efforts eventually seemed to amuse and please Tarr, and he began to teach Jaro more complicated lore. In due course a position opened for a junior mechanic; Jaro applied for the post and was hired. The work was arranged so that he would work as Tarr's assistant. During the summer he would work full time, and part time during the school term.

As Jaro had expected neither Luel nor Perseia Fath were pleased.

"It's truly senseless, Jaro," said Luel. "It can't be that you lack spending money; you have never yet used up the money that is set aside for you."

"That is true! You and Perseia are the most generous of parents; I've never lacked for anything. But I need to earn money for a special use."

"What use is that?" demanded Luel.

"As soon as I earn enough, I want to find out certain things about myself—where I came from, who was my mother, things of that sort. These questions worry me, and I won't rest until they are settled. But I don't want to use your money for what might be a wild goose chase."

Luel collected his thoughts. "I can see how these uncertainties must trouble you—but truly, Jaro, they are inconsequential in the total scope of your future. Before you set about any quest of this sort, complete your education. A degree at the Institute is prerequisite to a secure life. Without it, you are a will-o'-the-wisp or a vagabond, at the mercy of circumstances. It is time, and past time, that you settled upon a special course of studies; then, when your education is complete, you might consider these peripheral questions."

Luel paused. Jaro dared not mention the dreary voice at the back of his mind; Luel would instantly whisk him away to the psychiatrists, and Jaro wanted no more of their experiments.

Luel continued, his voice more stern: "I strongly urge that, for the present, you put aside this quest — which may or may not be quixotic. First things must come first. Your mother Perseia and I will help you without stint or question in your efforts to gain a proper education, of which we all may be proud, but we will resist any other course, as being against your best interests."

Perseia came into the room. Neither Luel nor Jaro wished to pursue the subject and it was dropped.

7.

Skirl called Jaro on the telephone and in a rather mysterious manner, arranged to meet him.

The meeting was secret, almost clandestine. Skirl seemed oddly excited. She described to Jaro the highly exclusive group known as the Quantarsi, whose goal was exploration of mystery, grandeur and beauty, and other topics as might seem worthy of comment. Quantarsi was so exclusive, in fact, that the only member was herself; all other applicants had, for one reason or another, been found wanting and rejected. Status was of no consequence and vagabonds, either of space or the spirit, would not be excluded on that account, although applicants must be clean, well-mannered, intelligent. As an afterthought Skirl added that they should not be ugly, tiresome, timid or talkative. She said that as she had sat musing over the admission requirements, the name 'Jaro' had surfaced into her mind and he was welcome to apply for membership, if he so desired. "Prestige, of course, is automatic," she told him, "since I am involved and we are fearfully exclusive."

Jaro agreed that there was nothing to lose. He applied for membership on the spot and was accepted.

They were sitting in Skirl's studio in the Hutsenreiter mansion on the slope of Nardessus Hill. The door flew open, to reveal the form of Dean Hutsenreiter. "What is going on?"

Jaro was surprised to find himself talking. "See for yourself."

Dean Hutsenreiter was taken aback. Then he said: "If I must accept insolence in my own house, I may as well go out and live in the street, where, at the very least, the expenses are less. Now then: who are you?"

Upon learning Jaro's almost non-existent social position, the dean ordered Jaro from the house and warned him never to annoy Skirl again with his importunities. Jaro departed with a humiliating lack of ceremony. He walked the two miles back to Merrihew, embarrassed, angry, scornful and amused by turns. He half-expected Skirl to telephone him, but there was no such communication and three days later he learned that Skirl had been packed off once more to her private school.

Chapter 2

1.

Jaro began his last term at the Lyceum. He continued to work part time at the spaceport, to the muted annoyance of Luel. "You are wasting time which could be put to better things," he told Jaro.

"I do it to earn money," said Jaro.

"Hmmf," said Luel. "You still have not given up your scheme?"

"I can't! There are things I need to know! Something is compelling me! Perhaps I am sensitive to thought voices."

"That is called 'telepathy'," said Luel. "I would hesitate to declare anything impossible — but more likely the fact that you do not know your origin predisposes you to restlessness."

"You should never feel any lack of security, or sense of place," Perseia assured him. "We feel as if you are our own son, and we are very proud of you."

"It is something more than insecurity," said Jaro. "Somewhere — somehow —" His voice trailed away. "Whatever it is, I must end this mystery."

"And so you shall," said Luel. "But first things first and by that I mean your education. When you have taken your degree and established an occupational niche for yourself, then you can take time for such a venture. But it would be irresponsible folly to think of such a quest before."

"But where did you find me? I want to know."

"All in good time," said Luel. "And then you shall know everything we know."

"You won't tell me now?"

"Please, Jaro! Don't insist!" cried Perseia. "If you had so much as a clue you might go kiting off like a crazy thing, and completely disrupt your education."

Luel said: "Believe us, Jaro, there is nothing we would not do for your benefit. That means we must have the strength of character to resist your appeals to help you do something wrong."

Perseia said: "You won't find any information in our records; we have altered all the significant information, since this, truly, is the only control we have over you, and we are determined that you should live a happy life. You will inherit all our investments, which are substantial, and naturally the house. This time, so we hope, is a long way off, but it is proper that you should know."

"Take your courses at the Institute so you will have a profession; then we will think about the mystery."

Emotion suffused Jaro. He ran up to his room, and sat staring from the window. He closed his eyes and ordered his thoughts. Luel and Perseia were right and it was wicked of him to think harshly of them. He must submerge his problems until he was free to deal with them on his own terms.

Jaro never brought up the subject again and his relations with the Faths resumed their old footing. He thought of them with affection; how could he resist their kindliness, generosity and sheer decency? Their only flaw, in his view, was a wry intellectual rationality, which in the main was too light-hearted to be really offensive. They made no secret of their affection for him. They also respected and admired him, since he displayed all their own virtues, along with the hard core of a quality which was not their own. They recognized it, but could give it no name. Obduracy? Inflexibility? Bitter courage? The quality was foreign to their own easy dispositions and sometimes it gave them pause. Jaro would be a very good friend, but a very bad enemy.

In order to please and reassure the Faths, Jaro dutifully applied himself to activities with what he considered an aesthetic orientation. He opted for a course at the Lyceum entitled 'Hellenistic Art of Ancient Earth' and he learned to play the socambar, a small resonating concertina with air pumped by a compact compressor. The instrument, once he got the sleight of it, enabled him to play popular lilts, jigs and saltarellos. Further, he tied a large ornamental rope mat of a thousand intricate parts. It was intended for the bathroom floor, but Perseia thought it far too fine and hung it on the wall over the fireplace.

Despite all, Luel remained unmollified, since Jaro was continuing his work, part time, at the spaceport, and now it seemed as if he felt reluctant to provide Jaro his former allowance. Jaro well understood the conflicts which worked upon Luel's mind, and realized that there could be no resolution with which Luel could take comfort, much less satisfaction, and Jaro felt much gloom on this account. His relationship with Evan Tarr continued as before. As the weeks became months, Jaro chanced upon certain odd inconsistencies in Tarr's background and in his accounts of himself. Jaro tactfully made no reference to them, though he was curious enough to devote several hours of research to the question of Tarr's provenance, which according to Tarr had been a farm near the town Kerloy, on the world Paltester. Jaro discovered some notable discrepancies, but was not disturbed; they might have any of a hundred explanations. Above all, they must not be made known to Luel, who would select the worst interpretation and become quite excited. Nor was Luel happy with Jaro's choice of the socambar as the instrument on which to excel. Luel described the socambar's tones as 'wheezes and grunts', though the 'amazing discords' to which he alluded might be due, so he conceded, to Jaro's execution of the complex fingerwork. Jaro, mortified, tried to make amends by agreeing to take a course in harmony.

Jaro was approaching the end of his time at the Lyceum, and he had a decision to make. Even though he worked full time during the summer, he would not have earned anywhere near enough funds for his purposes. Therefore, he could either continue to work full time, or he could start his advanced training at the Institute, though he still had not fixed upon any profession or special study for the long term. The Faths, of course, wanted him to enter the Institute. Jaro could not make up his mind.

Meanwhile life went on, with Jaro not at all pleased with the way his life was going, and as always the voice waxed and waned at the back of his consciousness, sometimes whimpering away into a misery too deep for lamentation; at other times, almost lucid in its sorrow. Jaro grimly submerged the voice by imagining himself playing a tune called 'The Felices d'Amour' on his socambar, over and over until the chords and sostenatos prevailed over the voice and in a mood of resentment almost palpable it desisted from its complaints.

Jaro had few acquaintances and no friends. His fellows thought him 'strange', 'morose', 'arrogant beyond his place'. Jaro barely noticed. His life went quietly; he felt no deprivations. The Faths provided him everything but what they themselves failed to enjoy: high social status. They had chosen to be part of a group which were sneeringly called 'Noops': folk who belonged to none of the social organizations. Currently, these ranged from Skirl's Quantarsi — so hyper-exclusive and ill-fated as to be non-existent — through the nearly as prestigious Clam Muffins (to which Skirl also belonged by virtue of her father's membership), then the Tattermen, the Scythians, and notably the 'Squared Circles'. These latter associations defined the social upper crust of the city, just underneath the quintessential Clam Muffins and Tattermen, with the Scythians considered a reckless and ambiguous group to the side of society. There were four 'Squared Circles', each quietly but definitely asserting its own preeminence, while half jocularly deploring the deficiencies of the rest. Each differed slightly from the others in tone and character. The Kahulibas included a few more financial magnates, while the Zookers tolerated an occasional discreetly unconventional sort, along with a few musicians and artists, and even a few discreet Scythians. The Naturals were dedicated to the refinements of decorous hedonism, while the Fugitives included many of the top faculty at the Thanet Institute. Still, all taken with all, there was little difference between any of the four, despite the sometimes rather shrill claims to supreme status, and a few incidents of hair-pullings, slapped faces, and the occasional suicide.

The Circles were anxious to recruit high-prestige new blood, but even more anxious to exclude outsiders and bounders. The Faths, members of the working faculty, though with considerable professional prestige, lacked social panache; as 'Noops' they were considered middle-class and even a bit tacky. Had either Luel or Perseia received trans-world honors, or mention in one of the journals published on Old Earth, then they might have fared better. The Faths were wryly amused, and cared little one way or the other, though for Jaro it came as a surprise to learn that his dear fosterparents, as 'Noops', were considered dull and devoid of the social graces.

When Jaro was about twelve he first noticed the patterns which controlled the behavior of his classmates. Luel Fath took time to explain the situation. "'Caste' and 'status' are not interchangeable words. 'Caste' is immutable; 'status' may change and sometimes can be controlled. They are both fascinating concepts, of great interest to the social scientist. You can't avoid them; they are universal. You swim in their influence as a fish swims in water. You have no choice but to adapt, as gracefully as possible."

"It seems peculiar, somehow."

"It isn't at all peculiar; in fact, it's quite natural and, arguably, serves a useful social purpose. Is it fair? Probably not, but what of that? Do you remember Baron Bodissey's* Thirteenth Axiom of Organized Existence?"

"Not exactly."

"As always he is terse. He asserts that only losers want fair play." Luel paused to consider. "The Baron is occasionally extravagant. A person surely can approve an act of justice without suffering remorse."

Jaro shrugged. "Fair or not, they can square a dozen circles a day, for all I care."

"Still, you should know what is going on," said Luel. "Remember, high society is exclusionary. You'll be barred with gusto and éclat unless someone finds it to his or her advantage to bring you in. Your own efforts to join would be futile and a source of happy amusement for all."

Jaro shrugged again. "I don't care a twitch, one way or the other."

---

* Unspiek, Baron Bodissey, a pantologist of Old Earth and elsewhere, had created a philosophical encyclopaedia, or compendium, of twelve volumes which he called simply LIFE, wherein he generalized upon the human condition. Baron Bodissey's oracular pronouncements tended to enrage lesser pundits, who found that Baron Bodissey had left them little leeway in which to exercise their quibbles and qualifications. Baron Bodissey was especially scathing in regard to what he called 'hyper-didacticism', meaning the employment of abstractions ten degrees removed from reality for the sake of intellectualism and rhetorical elegance. In a notable incident toward the end of his life he was excommunicated from the human race by the Society of Egalitarians at their All-Gaean Conclave at Venbenido on Canopus IV. Baron Bodissey's comment to this action was charged with significance, though it was succinct. He said: "The point is moot." To this day the most profound thinkers of the Gaean Reach are unable to agree upon the precise significance of the remark.

2.

Jaro was graduated from the Lyceum with honors. In the autumn he would enroll at the Institute, though he had not yet fixed upon an area of specialization. Like many of his classmates, he felt a wistful longing for work which would take him travelling far and wide, perhaps out on exploration of places still unknown. Unfortunately such careers were not mentioned in any of the employment information bulletins issued by the Institute Opportunity Offices. Jaro wondered about agronomical engineering, and also xeno-phytology, either of which might provide him freedom from a static existence.

Jaro had become a young man of good physique, spare, an inch or two taller than average, with a still, unobtrusive demeanor. His clear crisp features, the contrast between his dark hair and his pale olive-tan skin, his sternly erect posture produced an effect of innate if casual elegance. The Faths, pridefully taking note of his confident bearing and clean features sometimes wondered whether some noble house, somewhere in the Reach, might still be mourning the loss of a scion.

In the end Jaro enrolled himself at the Institute, in the field of Adaptive Agronomy: an occupation which would provide scope for travel.

During his first year at the Institute, Jaro encountered Lyssel Bynnoc, the daughter of a prominent financier. She was a year or two younger than himself and a member of the Kahulibah Circle. Lyssel was slight and flexible, and often seemed to squirm with the unruly energy of a small affectionate animal. Lyssel was neither good nor bad; such concepts were incommensurable when used in connection with Lyssel. Her body was that of a young nymph. In repose, her face was pretty enough, though a bit thin and wistful-seeming, but it was seldom in repose, so that the effect was one of electrifying and fascinating vitality. Her hair was a nondescript dusty-blonde tangle growing low over her forehead, back over and past her ears. Her jaw and chin seemed fragile, with slanting cheeks and a wide mouth, always restless, quirking up and down at the corners, twisting to the butterfly flutter of her thoughts. What with her wry grimaces and extravagant attitudes,

Lyssel was hard to dislodge from the imagination once she had secured a beachhead. Rumors regarding Lyssel were everywhere rife, such as: 'I've just come from the fountain where Kildy Blomberk is rhapsodizing about Lyssel. He says she is like the pure and delicate flower of the legend which fades and collapses after pollination. Franchei Dydenbeck told him that it was a beautiful thought, but that Lyssel was probably more durable than the flower of legend, and if any such pollination had occurred, Lyssel seemed none the worse for it.'

Lyssel had a taste for foolishness nor was she averse to mischief, if any were in the offing. Girls her own age were wary of her and in her company felt like frumps. The boys, however, were fascinated and she was the topic of endless speculation. Just how much of her feckless irresponsibility was a pose and how much was real? No one, so it seemed, had ever learned the truth, though many had given the problem their serious attention, especially a certain Hanfer Irmerankin, another member of the Kahulibahs.

Jaro encountered Lyssel in a science laboratory, and was favorably impressed, though in a spirit of detachment, since, as usual, he was preoccupied with his own affairs. Lyssel, in her turn noticed the tall dark-haired youth with the pensive expression. She felt his attention and turned away, expecting him to approach on one pretext or another, but when she looked around he was busy with his work.

Hmm, thought Lyssel. She appraised him covertly. In a quiet and unobtrusive way he was quite attractive. His features were well shaped, even rather aristocratic. She wondered whether he might be an offworlder. It was quite possible, she thought. Of course, like all the other boys she knew, he'd be putty in her grasp — once she got her hands on him. It seemed a good idea. Hanfer Irmerankin would be annoyed, of course, which was all to the good.

Hanfer was indeed irked when she mentioned Jaro and described his virtues. "He has a very interesting look, as if he were a landed grandee, or perhaps one of the Overmen from Dambrosilla. There's some sort of mystery about him; at least, that's the rumor."

"Bah!" sneered Hanfer, a large, rather heavy youth with bold features, including a long nose of which he was proud and which, in his opinion, lent him a noble and commanding profile. He wore his blond hair after the new and daring fashion, sweeping over his fine broad forehead then back and off to the side. He scoffed at Lyssel's reference to Jaro. "You're talking sheer bullypup! There's no mystery about the fellow! He's an absolute moop: a nobody; I can't see why you trouble to notice him!"

Lyssel spoke flippantly: "He's said to be quite intelligent, and a musical virtuoso."

Lyssel's grandiloquence was intended to tease and infuriate Hanfer, and was based upon a half-heard remark to the effect that Jaro had been seen playing the socambar at a lyceum picnic.

"No matter; he can be the Third Coming of four-toed Gezemyer, for all I care. He's not in the Circles, and that's what counts in my book."

"Hanfer, you really are extreme. I'm sorry that I must tell you this, but it's true. The Circles are not everything in life."

"Ha hah! The Circles may not be everything, but they separate quality from schmeltzers, bounders and moops."

"Jaro is nothing of the sort!" declared Lyssel. "Be good enough to speak politely of my friends!"

"Certainly, when they deserve it. This fellow whatever-his-name is a gak and a peeker, and if he starts smelling around you, I'll have a word with him."

"Well, you might as well know! I've invited him to the lawn party, and if you're not nice, I will be furious with you."

3.

'Society without ritual is like music played on a single-stringed instrument with one finger'. Such was the dictum of Unspiek, Baron Bodissey.

At Thanet trivial considerations might place one family, or an individual, higher or lower in the social gradation than another of seemingly equivalent attributes. At Thanet especially there was no equality, every one occupied a stage different from every other family or individual. No one, not even the Faths, could be indifferent to his or her place in the social structure. Everyone was a social arbiter; eyes were vigilant, ears listened for what should not have been said. A moment's lapse, a tactless remark, an absent-minded glance interpreted as arrogance, might generate days or weeks or months of discomfort and discord. To presume to an elevated status, or 'getting beyond one's self' was a transgression which often incurred sharp rebuffs. Status, so it was felt, was a precious commodity that bounders must not be allowed to preempt.

The Faths enjoyed moderately high status by reason of their occupation; Jaro shared this status, though he was almost oblivious to its existence. So it was that when Lyssel, the daughter of a financial magnate, and a Kahuliba, invited Jaro to the garden party, he accepted the invitation without a second thought. At the party he was taken aside by a glowering young man named Hanfer Irmerankin, and warned away from Lyssel; she was, so Hanfer declared, his own special interest, and Jaro was a damnable 'schmeltzer'* who had better mind his manners. Lyssel upbraided Hanfer, and instructed Jaro to ignore the uncouth remarks. Hanfer, so she assured Jaro, had no right to interfere in her choice of associates.

Jaro shrugged and followed her advice. The festivities of the day continued while Hanfer glowered from the side and presently departed, to Jaro's relief; he had half-anticipated further remonstrances.

Two days later, at midnight, as Jaro returned home from a lecture, he was waylaid by four 'Angels of Vengeance': four masked individuals wearing costumes of dread: black capes draped over a frame to suggest abnormally wide shoulders, grotesque masks, odd boots with long pointed toes. The four set upon Jaro, bore him to the ground. Into Jaro's mind came a vivid flash of recollection; he lay in the dirt with the Wyching Hills behind, as terrible blows thudded down upon him. Amazing! Even while his flesh cringed to the blows, from inside his head came a gust of mocking humorless laughter, as if somewhere something took joy in the event.

The blows were dealt with flexible truncheons, and struck with no great ferocity, their intent being to punish and intimidate rather than to harm. Presently the beating came to an end. A hoarse voice spoke in labored groaning tones: "Thus is punishment dealt to schmeltzers! Let them beware!"

---

* Note: There is no exact contemporary rendition of the verb 'schmeltz'. The approximate meaning is: 'To filch status beyond one's right'.

From the others came a rumbling chanted chorus: "It is always thus!"

The deep voice spoke again: "You are a schmeltzer. Say you are sorry!"

Jaro tried to gain his feet, but was thrust back down and kicked. Again: "Admit your falsity! Say you are sorry and will keep to your place! Speak!"

Jaro tried to struggle, but was held down while his hair was clipped from his head.

"So the Angels of Death deal with gaks, cads, vulgarians and schmeltzers, who encroach upon persons too good for them! Say that you are sorry."

Jaro tried to crawl to the side, but the figure towering above kicked him in the ribs. "Quick now! Abase yourself!"

There were further blows and kicks, now vicious and desperate. Jaro again knew the dry taste of dirt and a sickening sense of failure and defeat. His senses began to drain away; once more he heard the chuckle of sardonic amusement from the source so close within, yet so far apart. He lay limp. It was good, this inertness; he felt like a reservoir, collecting a fury of purpose he had not known before.

The 'Angels' tired of their exercise, and after a few final kicks, more in the nature of afterthoughts than as vehicles of correction, they trotted off, well pleased with their success. They had punished a schmeltzer; they had restored order to the complicated harmonies of Thanet's social structure. It was a good night's work, especially since they had enjoyed the exercise without anyone learning their identity.

Jaro limped home, thoughtful and not as excited as Luel became when he saw him. "What happened?"

Jaro explained in a matter-of-fact voice.

"Can you name these hooligans?"

"Oh indeed. Hanfer Irmerankin, Aubry Cudd, Jehame Wistenor, Kocson Herdy."

"Then we will prosecute."

Jaro would not hear of it. "Nothing would be gained. I could prove nothing. There were no witnesses. The Justiciary would never inflict high-status folk to the truth machine. Even if they were deemed guilty, they would only be censured, and I would be warned to avoid provocative acts. Who would win? They would emerge with dignity. I would look feeble and foolish."

"But we cannot let this outrage pass! It would be shameful!"

"Yes; indeed it would."

Luel surveyed him in amazement: "You show no emotion!"

Jaro smiled. "I never show emotion. But yes, I am angry. I can barely control it. But I want to use the anger. I cannot waste it. I am lucky that it has come upon me."

Luel shook his head. "I don't understand you."

Jaro spoke pensively: "Do you remember Evan Tarr?"

"Yes, naturally! What of Evan Tarr?"

"One day he happened to mention his scars; then he spoke of combat and fighting. He told me that he could teach me, when I was ready to learn. Now I am ready."

Luel thought for a moment, then said: "He is a man of violence. I can read the signs in his face. He has lived much of his life in dangerous places, of his own accord, which to me indicates that he has small reverence for human life and cares little for human pain. Evan Tarr, I frankly admit, frightens me."

Jaro smiled. "I know him better than that. He can teach me what I need to know."

Luel again was silent, then blurted: "Perhaps this is the wrong time to make careful ethical distinctions. You have been hurt; make no mistake: I am as angry as you! But I want to take revenge through the designated channels of social accommodation. These are proper and permitted; in short, they are civilized. I don't want you to do violent illegal deeds, as if you were a space vagabond or a pirate of the Beyond."

Jaro said at last: "I was attacked. I could not respond. I lay on the ground. I would be wrong to let it happen again."

Luel stared at him, then made a small hopeless gesture of pain and defeat, and turned away.

Two days later Jaro met Evan Tarr during the evening. He gave a terse description of the Angels of Death and their activities. Evan Tarr listened impassively, then asked: "Do you know these people?"

"Yes, but it is not important. In a way, they have done me a favor, so I forgive them."

"That is a kindly impulse."

"Perhaps. Now I am angry—and awake. I want to learn what you can teach me. Naturally, I will pay for your time."

Evan Tarr approached. He inspected Jaro's bruises, then felt Jaro's biceps and shoulders. "Your tone is good. There is an elasticity to you and you have strong wrists. You should do very well. There need be no talk of payment. How much do you want me to teach you?"

"As much as you can, and as much as I can learn."

"I can teach a great deal. It is one of my special skills; in fact, I was taught by the Grand Masters of the art."

"Indeed! Where was that?"

"It's a long story: too long to be told at this time. Now then, you must be aware that it is hard and it is uncomfortable."

"No matter. It is why I have saved my anger."

Evan Tarr smiled his twisted smile. "So it shall be."

Jaro had already returned to his routine at the Institute, ignoring the stares of his fellows. At noon of the first day, Lyssel approached and looked him over dispassionately. "They did a fine job upon you. It was not nice, and now, of course, you are shamed." She was half smiling, but there was coolness in her manner.

"Yes, in a way. In another way: no."

"What an odd thing to say! Is there a secret meaning concealed in the remark?"

"It's too complicated to explain."

Lyssel's smile became even more chilly. "You are a strange person, Jaro Fath. You walk back and forth as if nothing had happened, when everyone knows you were shamed. Have you no pride?"

"Why do you ask?"

"You show yourself in public, like a whipped dog smiling and curling its lip to beg for tolerance."

Jaro grimaced. "I will try to look less servile and doglike; but think: is it possible that I am appearing in public because I have a class at this hour?"

Lyssel's jaw dropped. "Are you telling me that your class is more urgent to you than your dignity?"

Jaro reflected. "I don't think that is what I said."

"You are explaining that you don't care who sees you? That you don't care what anyone thinks?"

Jaro nodded. "That is almost correct."

Lyssel gave her head a jerk which sent her tawny curls flying. "I suppose that you include me in this group? I don't think it's considerate of you."

"Hm," said Jaro. "This becomes more complicated by the minute. You think that I should avoid my classes as a courtesy to you?"

Lyssel nodded. "It would be better and nicer, and far less embarrassing for me."

"Sorry," said Jaro. "It can't be done!"

Lyssel pouted. "I don't understand you, Jaro, not at all! But I don't think that I like you."

Hanfer Irmerankin approached, a ropy grin of rather sinister import on his broad pink face. "I thought you had been warned away from the upper turf, schmeltzer."

Lyssel said quickly: "Come now, Hanfer! Don't be unpleasant; Jaro means nothing wrong."

"Bah," said Hanfer. "He means nothing whatever. He smiles meekly; he licks his lips; he is not even annoyed."

"Wrong," said Jaro. "I am annoyed, but it is like a tonic or an elixir which I cannot waste upon you."

"You talk foolishness, like a popinjay or a clown. I don't understand you; that's a fact. Perhaps you are mad."

Jaro turned away and later, when he began learning from Evan Tarr, he set himself to the first exercises and disciplines with a zeal which surprised Tarr, so much that he uttered a caution. "Slow down! You'll burn yourself out!"

"I'm sure not," said Jaro. "I need only let Hanfer Irmerankin explain his opinion of me. He enjoys it and I profit by the opportunity it gives me to practice self-control and a thick skin to shame."

Evan Tarr merely grunted, then said: "Sit down over here and I'll trim your hair. It's better to have it all short than growing out in tufts."

Three months later the term ended. During the winter recess Luel and Perseia went off on an expedition to the Molcanes Islands on the world Lakhmi Verde, by the star Virgo KKA-933, where they revelled in a tinkling music of gongs, bells, whistles and flutes.

In due course the new term at the Lyceum began. On the third day Jaro chanced upon Lyssel as she crossed the terrace in front of the main structure. He turned and waited as she approached. For a time it seemed as if she would pass by without taking notice of him; then, at the last minute, she paused and turned her head. "It's Jaro, isn't it?"

"Yes! I am Jaro. Do you not recognize me?"

"I know hundreds, even thousands, of people," said Lyssel. "Some are more similar than others. Some are the most similar of all."

"I hope you include me in that last group," said Jaro. "I like not being noticed."

"Much depends on how you behave," said Lyssel.

"In that case, look at me now, so that you will know me next time. I have changed, of course. My welts and bruises have healed; my hair has grown out; my dignity is on the mend. Do you still despise me?"

Lyssel laughed gaily. "What an odd question! Do you want the truth?"

"Certainly; why not?"

"In that case, listen and be abashed! Because it is not fair that a person of your minimal social level should look so naturally aristocratic. Don't you feel nervous, or even deceitful?"

"For all you know, I am indeed an aristocrat."

Lyssel looked at him in wonder. "How can that be? The Faths are not even Countryflyers, or Arimaspians —" here Lyssel named two unpretentious rural social organizations. "You've never even joined the athletic club."

"True," said Jaro. "I admit that I am a vagabond. Still, I can't help how I look."

"That is part of the attraction. Mind you, I am not referring to Jaro Fath the person, but the symbolic impact of your appearance — which is quite high class."

"So: you despise the living seething passionate Jaro but not the Jaro-like surface that reflects sanitary light rays into your eyes and fools you."

Lyssel tried to control her smiling. "I've never noticed any wild seething passion in the first Jaro."

"Both Jaros so far have shown good sense. Neither wants to be snubbed. Have I been too timid?"

Lyssel changed the subject. "I don't know whether I can stand another term at school. I do so love our place at Blue Mountain Lake! Believe me, Jaro, it was not all parties and swimming and games! I worked hard; you'd have been surprised! I helped in the fire-bark harvest and gathered four pecks of tankberries. Right now I am still half dizzy with the stress of returning to school. So really, I haven't thought of you for ages, one way or another. For this you should be grateful, or so I suppose."

"How so?"

"It is that foolish Hanfer," said Lyssel lightly. "He still becomes furious whenever your name comes up. He thinks that I have some odd secret regard for you, which he finds deplorable."

"And how deep is this regard?"

Lyssel threw her hand out in an extravagant gesture, as if she were flinging gold coins to a multitude of paupers. "It is quite small, though I mention you occasionally in order to keep Hanfer in his place."

"The logic of all this eludes me."

"No matter; who cares a fig for logic? Not I! Truthfully, Jaro, you mystify me. I can't believe that you are as meek as you want me to believe."

"Well — naturally I don't want to alarm Hanfer. He has helped me more than he will ever know."

"That sounds most wildly irrational," said Lyssel brightly. "On the other hand, I suppose you mean something sensible, even though I have not the shadow of a notion what."

"No matter, and look! There is Hanfer himself! He is scowling in this direction."

"Then you had better leave."

"Not just yet."

Hanfer stood nearby in company with several friends, with whom he was arranging an excursion for the following weekend. At the sight of Jaro his face had become twisted and he called out: "Hoy there, schmeltzer! You don't seem able to learn! So, cut your stick and hop off on the double, like the good little strankenpus you are."

Jaro said to Lyssel: "The time has arrived. Hanfer at last has become intolerable."

Lyssel laughed. "Hanfer has always been intolerable. He hasn't really changed, and since he is inclined to want his own way, you'd be wise simply to avoid him."

"There's a better way." Jaro put his arms around Lyssel and kissed her. She grinned up at him. "That would have been nicer if it had not been done to spite Hanfer."

Jaro kissed her again. "That was for real, since I was already out of sorts."

Hanfer took a step toward Jaro, then halted and turned away.

Jaro started to kiss Lyssel again, but she held him off. "That is not the way to remain unobtrusive."

"Nowadays I don't care much, one way or the other."

Lyssel still held him off. "Look! Hanfer is strolling away! That is mystifying, since he is known for his brusque temperament. I wonder what he has in mind." She considered a moment, watching Jaro sidelong. "I think that you might have hurt poor Hanfer's feelings."

Jaro looked after Hanfer's retreating broad back. "I suppose it's possible."

Lyssel reflected, then with the breathless air of one about to perform a daring feat — she said: "Tonight at Fan Hall my cousin is playing the dombrilian. It will be a dull affair; still I am expected to show myself. You might like to be on hand, as well — to keep me amused."

"It sounds very nice."

"Then I'll see you there?"

Jaro shook his head. "I have an appointment I can't put off."

"Come after your appointment."

Jaro smiled sadly. "I don't know how long the business will take."

Lyssel tossed her head. "Sometimes I think that you do not hold me in the proper regard."

"Not true!" Jaro tried again to kiss her, but she drew away. "Tonight, you can kiss your 'business associate' until her ridiculous ears drop off."

4.

In the morning there was news of a most curious and even inexplicable event. Hanfer Irmerankin and three of his friends, dressed as 'Angels of Merciful Death' had been discovered beside a country road, all suffering grievously from broken bones, multiple fractures, bruises and contusions. Further, they had been carrying a quantity of depilatory compound; this substance had been smeared over their own heads, with the result that all were now stone bald. Apparently they had been out on a lark when they had been attacked by a gang of hoodlums. Their injuries were not only painful and debilitating, but seemed also to demoralize the limp victims. None, when finally able to talk, chose to discuss the episode except in husky whispers. The police refused to investigate, since, as 'Angels of Merciful Death', the four had evidently been engaged upon illicit mischief. So there the matter rested. As for Lyssel, she avoided Jaro for most of the day, and only late in the afternoon was he able to approach her. Even then, she turned quickly away.

"Wait!" cried Jaro. "Where are you going?"

Lyssel shrugged. "Anywhere else but here."

"Can I come with you?"

"No."

"That is hardly polite."

Lyssel eyed him stonily. "Since when have you troubled with politeness?"

"At this moment, if at no other time."

"It is a welcome change." Lyssel swung her eyes away. "Still, I must be going." She darted him a glance. "And you, of course, have your various secrets to attend to. Also, you must not neglect to pay off your gang."

"Gang? The only gang was Hanfer's gang of Angels which jumped on me from out of the bushes. I was alone."

Lyssel stared in disbelief. "That can't be true! Hanfer said there were six! That is surely more reasonable. You are not telling the truth, and I can't abide liars!"

Lyssel marched away. Jaro watched her retreating figure with sadness. He listened; the internal voice gave a choked sardonic gurgle: the caricature of a laugh. Jaro smiled grimly. "Laugh then, idiotic hidden voice! Laugh as you like; you will not affect me."

Lyssel would never be part of his life: he could tell himself this and feel an ease in the telling of it to himself. The croaking laughter dwindled and lapsed to a mindless gurgle. "If in truth this is my alter ego, and I am a multiple personality, I only hope I can keep this influence at bay. With all my soul and strength I will resist!"

He wondered whether he should confide in Evan Tarr, but decided against the step. So far, only Skirl Hutsenreiter had learned of his problems, and a new thought entered his mind: a fragment of gossip, to the effect that Skirl had returned to Thanet. She had been expelled from her private school, or perhaps Dean Hutsenreiter had not paid the fees; at any rate Skirl was back in town.

5.

A week later Luel reported that he had received a casual offer for the house and acreage, from a real estate magnate named Norby Mildoon. The offer had not been tempting, but neither Luel nor Perseia had any exaggerated notions as to the value of ramshackle old Merrihew and its fifty acres of hinterland. "Still," said Perseia, "it's a very pleasant home for the three of us; it's quiet and peaceful and we can hear the wind in the trees instead of traffic in the streets."

"That all may change, if anyone starts a development along Gwendolyne Road," said Luel gloomily. "For years I've heard rumors of industrial complexes and country clubs and even a satellite town, practically in our front yard."

"That's all just talk, except maybe for the country club," said Perseia. "Thanet is growing toward the east and the south, not out in this direction."

"That may be true," said Luel. "Still, it's also true that Merrihew is slowly falling apart. The roof leaks; we need new windows in the kitchen, the timber should be treated with Constor. It all means money, time and effort, and what do we have in the end? A cranky old farm house with floors out of level and every wall askew. Sooner or later,

Jaro will be going off on his own, and we'll be left to rattle around in an untidy old barn."

Perseia looked at Luel in surprise. "I've never heard you speak this way before!"

"I suppose I'm in a bit of a bad mood."

"Personally, I'm fond of the old place. I wouldn't want to sell until there was some reason to do so — especially not at Mildoon's price."

"You're right, of course. Just so long as you don't insist that I paint the place from a ladder."

Chapter 3

1.

By chance Jaro came upon Skirl in the Institute library. She had changed little, he thought; she was still active, quick, self-assured; her short dark hair still clasped her face like a casque; her body was still taut and trim; she still carried herself with that hint of swaggering reckless gallantry associated with fairy princes and princesses in the course of their adventures. She dressed as before, to suit herself, without concern for style or show, too proud to care for appearances. Jaro watched her a moment or two from across the room. She did not appear particularly happy. He started to turn away, but she raised her eyes and saw him, and it was too late. He crossed the room and sat down beside her. "I heard you were back in Thanet."

"Yes. For a time, at least."

"Are you studying at the Institute?"

Skirl laughed, at the ridiculous suggestion. "Of course not."

"What are you doing here?"

Skirl looked down at the books and pamphlets on the table. "I must go somewhere, as soon as I can — in another year. I am trying to decide where." She frowned down at the pamphlet on the table in front of her: an index to the library information system. "There are many places to go."

"What will you do after you get there?"

"I don't know. It all depends upon where 'there' is. I must think the matter out carefully, since I'll have no money from my father, and I don't want to live in poverty, either sordid or otherwise."

"Does your father know of your plans?"

Skirl gave her head a sad shake. "My poor father! He is remodelling our house and he can't pay for it. I think he is trying for a loan at Institute Bank."

Jaro was silent a moment.

"The Faths are going off to a Grand Conclave of Xenologists at Dimplewater on the world Ushan. They mentioned that your father would also be on hand."

"Yes. He is one of the principal speakers."

"Are you going with him?"

"No."

"Nor I; in fact, I'll be alone at Merrihew while they are gone. Will you come to visit me?"

Skirl looked at him, scowling in perplexity. "At the moment I can't think of any reason to do so."

"Nor I, for a fact."

"Then why did you ask?"

"I don't know. It was an act of daring folly."

Skirl shrugged. "If I get bored I might look in."

2.

The Faths went off on a combination holiday/study tour to the world Ushan. At Dimplebury, the City of a Thousand Bridges, they would attend a Grand Conclave of Xenologists — a category which included almost every variety of philosopher, explorer, philologer, lexicographer, cartologist, historian and a dozen other more recondite professions, the emphasis at the Conclave being upon Social Analysis.

Before departure, the Faths told Jaro something of Ushan and the city Dimplewater. "Scenically it is said to be an absolute paradise, with canals everywhere, and trees overhanging the water. The residences are like small palaces; there is no poverty nor deprivation. The folk are intelligent, highly civilized and handsome; they realize that they are living a golden existence. In the country almost everyone has some sort of isolated cottage, where he can enjoy the solitude, which — oddly enough — is an aspect of the Ushan psyche. They are not a gregarious folk; each person lives as if he were an island, and why? The answer seems to be that in the pleasant environment there is no need for social support, and the intrusion of other folk into one's affairs is a bother. Therefore each lives his 'tamsour'."

Jaro asked: "What is 'tamsour'?"

"It is untranslatable. It would appear to mean the total experience of one's life, as if it were condensed into a single drop of essence, or exemplified by a single symbol, or a single moment of profound enlightenment. Of course, this is not the case; these symbols do not exist, nor even the words adequately to express 'tamsour'."

Jaro mused: "Perhaps it would be the secret meaning of one's life, with the denouement supplied by the voice of Fate. That, of course, is a metaphysical concept."

"True. But where is the exact boundary between 'metaphysics' and 'physics'? No one has ever provided a satisfactory definition."

"No one has ever trisected an angle or squared a circle, either."

Luel laughed. " 'Tamsour' is something like 'fate', but specific to each individual, and flavored with a secret essence which only he or she knows. According to the Ushan ideas, you have your 'tamsour' and I have mine, each unique and, by the Ushan reckoning, antipathetic and corrosive, should they chance to impinge one on the other."

"They would seem to be trained to extreme egocentricity."

"Quite so, though this is over-simplification. There is no social friction on Ushan; there are no classes nor caste patterns — at least none the casual visitor can detect, though — just as everywhere else, they probably exist."

"It sounds rather strange. I'm not sure I would want to live there. Are there no criminals?"

"Every society has its mix of typical crimes. Here on Gallingale we have slander, blackmail, defamation of character, financial crimes for the sake of augmenting wealth and status. On Ushan these offenses are unknown. The society is like a quantity of radioactive material; at random and unknown intervals one of its atoms explodes in a great spasm of energy. He celebrates, or blames, his tamsour. Self-pity is involved. It is a peculiar and special form of amok, during which the over-stressed individual self-destructs, as dramatically and poetically as possible. The episode always arouses wide critical interest and is discussed in murmurs of analysis and appreciation, or if the performance is bad — amusement and disgust. The act is uncommon, but not rare; perhaps one person in fifty feels strongly enough about his tamsour to so dedicate his being."

"Odd. Even extraordinary."

"Ha!" said Luel. "Every aspect of existence is odd and extraordinary. Have you forgotten your own origins?"

"Yes, and no. I can't forget something I have never known. But I have not forgotten that some day I must set myself to learning."

"All in good time," said Luel. "Meanwhile, I wish you were coming to Ushan with us."

"I don't think I would feel comfortable in that sort of atmosphere."

Luel gave a rueful laugh. "You haven't heard the worst of it. Sometimes the death-seeker gathers quantities of beautiful goods: rugs, porcelains, rare wood filigrees, bibelots, ancient curios. Often he heartlessly confiscates such precious objects from his friends and neighbors, taking care to seize their most treasured possessions. He heaps these priceless objects around a central pylon and sets them ablaze, dancing a jig on a high platform singing out his own requiem. Listen: this is one of such declamations which was recorded." Luel touched a button and a sonorous voice cried out: "Here I stand, the darling of time, the king of light, the soul of love and joy, the blissful, precious and beloved core of all being! I cry out against injustice; it is rampant in the Cosmos; it is the great Devil! It fosters death, but first it creates life in the form of myself to appreciate that which it intends to kill; is this not injustice? I am the God of Life, but I must die and know the end of all good things! So be it! I die if not in victory, at least in the glory of my tamsour! If the cosmos thinks to play this tragic joke upon me, the cosmos shall suffer more than I, since I go out in a suffusion of beauty! This smoke I breathe, it is like incense; I am intoxicated with the beauty of my going! Let the cosmos beware! The future is blank; when I am gone a voice remains; who then shall the Arch-devil torment? I shall glory in my sunset colors of death! I will be famed for my great tamsour! Now behold: I soar from my place on high; I fly in utter grace and parabolic elegance to the end of all!"

The voice ended. Another voice said without emphasis: "The gentleman Varvis Malapan has just plunged a hundred feet to his death, and so has consummated his tamsour. He is no more, and the cosmos he ruled has become oblivion."

Luel and Perseia Fath travelled aboard the great spacepacket *Shahambre Traveller* to the spaceport at Daphne Stranway on the world Ushan, then rode by air transport to Dimplewater across the continent.

Dimplewater had prepared for the Grand Conclave of Xenology, the Humanic Arts and Sciences with debonair and effortless ease. The principal venue was the rotunda of the Waterfairy Hotel: a hemisphere constructed entirely of irregular panes of colored glass, in a black iron web. From the apex hung a remarkable light source: a sphere twenty feet in diameter constructed of smaller segments of colored glass, glowing with entrancing light, like back-lit rubies, sapphires, emeralds. The hotel proper connected through an arch: first a lobby intersected by four canals, where guests might embark aboard water-taxis for any area of Dimplewater. The residential chambers occupied a succession of rings above the lobby. It was quite the most entrancing hostelry of any in the experience of either Luel or Perseia. Staff had been recruited from off-world; the local folk were either too affluent or too dignified to engage in such work,

Luel and Perseia arrived at the hotel a day early, and found an opportunity to lunch with Nian Murrevil, the chairman of the arrangements committee. Nian Murrevil, like other citizens of Ushan, was slender, spare, of good physique, with dark hair growing low from a wide forehead, large dark hazel eyes, a long straight nose and a wide well-shaped mouth, of a sort which might have been called 'sensual', though probably with no great justification. Nian Murrevil was possibly ten years older than Luel Fath, and behaved in a most engaging manner.

Perseia inquired: "I've been looking down the list, and I don't see any local names save your own. Are there no scholars in the field on Ushan?"

"Not many," said Nian Murrevil. "For one reason or another our really notable scholars go off-world to study and take their honors, and are diffident about returning. We are not particularly apt at theorizing or abstract studies; for instance, while we have many outstanding musicians, we have no musicologists."

"Interesting," said Luel. "May I ask a personal question?"

Nian Murrevil smiled politely. "Of course."

"You are wearing on the epaulette of your jacket a set of small devices, which looks like recording equipment. What is their purpose?"

Nian Murrevil's smile became a trifle thin. "The explanation is rather complex; with me, the devices are no more than a habit since I do not take their purpose seriously."

"And as for that purpose?"

Nian Murrevil shrugged. "Folk since time immemorial have kept journals and diaries for themselves. These devices serve that purpose. They record the events of one's life, and are excellent reference sources should someone forget an important fact or an appointment."

"But how do you deal with such a volume of information?"

Again Nian Murrevil shrugged. "We usually set aside a few moments of each day to review the events of the previous day, so that we can organize them. In short, we extract material, pleasant or otherwise, which deserves preservation; the rest is discarded. It is a perhaps an obsessive habit, but for some reason we cannot break it. Now you must excuse me. I have enjoyed our meeting and will certainly cherish it among my mementos." Nian Murrevil departed.

Luel looked after him. "Amazing folk, these Mordeanos. Do you know what I think?"

"Probably," said Perseia. "Say it anyway."

"These folk are troubled by the fact that each moment of their lives comes, goes and never returns. The wheel of Time rolls and with every revolution grinds away their existence and reduces the scope for a glorious 'tamsour'. I may or may not be using the word correctly."

"Hmf," sniffed Perseia. "No one cares whether I have a nice tamsour or not."

"You won't get much sympathy on Ushan. They are worried about themselves. They begrudge each passing moment unless it affords them exaltation of a high order, or something similar."

Perseia gave a rueful laugh. "Nian Murrevil wasted precious little time on us. We failed to exhilarate him."

Luel said: "Next time I will dip into my repertory of backroom jokes."

"And I will dance the kazatzka."

On the following day the participants at the conference assembled in the rotunda: a group of scholars, scientists and academicians to the number of five hundred. Some had brought papers they intended to read; others would merely listen and engage in the important work of intellectual cross-fertilization. Nian Murrevil was chairman and interlocutor. An hour after noon, he called to order the first session of the conference. He made a brief opening statement, then threw the conference open to the presentation of scholarly papers. "Ladies and gentlemen, we will now hear the distinguished Sir Paul Piatky."

Sir Paul stepped forward: a sturdy gentlemen with a high brush of coarse black hair. His flamboyant garments offered a host of sartorial symbols distinctly at odds with his melancholy countenance. In a burst of insight Perseia told Luel that Sir Paul had been forced to wear the garments at the behest of his wife, which also explained his dour expression.

Sir Paul's message was also cheerless. "The societies of the Gaean Reach are now so complex, disparate and scattered so far, deep and wide that we can no longer think in terms of comprehensive scholarship, sublime though that notion might have seemed to our forebears. To express my thesis more broadly, the volume of knowledge has grown ten times faster than our ability to classify, much less understand, it.

"This is a bleak prospect for the future, as well everyone in this august audience recognizes. The basic purport is that our careers are demonstrably exercises in futility, and the conscientious among us will henceforth accept our salaries with a grimace of guilt. The time has come for us to alter our perspectives and to become realists, rather than academic fossils, dreaming of a past age of innocence.

"So — what now? Is all lost? Not necessarily. Our field of expertise, as redefined, becomes simply taxonomic. No longer will we collate, analyze, synthesize, and search for felicitous correspondences. Our cherished and delightful laws of social dynamics must be relegated to the same box as the theory of Phlogiston. Now we are realists! Even so, we will be hard-put even to keep abreast of new information, much less analyze it. Why delude ourselves?"

A florid man in the front row jumped to his feet. He called out a reply to what Sir Paul had intended as a rhetorical question. "Obviously, to keep our jobs!"

Sir Paul turned a haughty glance down at the florid man and continued. "There are at least two routes past the seeming impasse. First: we can arbitrarily nominate a number of settled worlds — let us say, thirty or even forty, or even fifty and declare these worlds the only suitable arena for serious study. In so doing, we ignore all other human activity, no matter how astounding. Is it tragic? Or sensational? Or rife with human drama? We care nothing; we elbow the unwelcome information to the side! We tremble at no enormity! After all, we are the authorities, so we tell our students, and we know best. The so-called 'control group' of worlds with their readily accessible cultures will provide a manageable range of data, and each of us may vote for the inclusion of his favorite world. By this means, we maintain the dignity and repute of the profession. Our studies are as profound as we like and we are all eminently comfortable. Meanwhile, our students learn the rudiments of cultural anthropology, which they can apply as they see fit. If mavericks or mad geniuses among our group choose to study other societies, let them do so; it is all one to us. We simply laugh them to the side, and as we control the grants, tenures and salaries, they quickly come to heel."

"Preposterous!" called the florid man in the front row. "What an imbecilic notion!"

As before, Sir Paul paid the gentleman no heed. "The second concept is more complicated. We assemble a gigantic information-bank — a data-processing apparatus of unprecedented scope. Our task then alters; we merely collect information and feed it into this mechanism without piddling or toodling with the details, as if we knew what we were doing. The machine accepts the information in a raw state, unclassified, undigested, unanalyzed. That is all there is to it. The machine has been programmed to collate and rationalize. Our lives have become tranquil. As we sit chatting in our clubs, drinking beverages of choice, a subject might arise in which we take a casual interest, or perhaps we wish to settle a bet. In the bad old times — by that, I mean now — we would be forced to exert ourselves. By the new system, we merely reach out a hand, touch a button, and the relevant information is provided on the instant. We are no longer paltry underpaid low-status academics; we have started to live the good life. We no longer distinguish ourselves by our former constricted field; now we are Doctors of Erudition? It is, I am assured, a glorious prospect.

"Now then: a final word. Certain smug boffins whose names I will not mention — though I can see their hangdog grins from where I stand — would boom and huffaw to their tenure committees as slavishly as ever, but — aha, and here is the great joke! — we sit on the committee!"

"Bah!" sneered the florid gentleman in the front row. "If your idiotic scheme were in force, what else are we good for?"

"You can sell your corpse for pet food," said Sir Paul. "Also, that of your wife if such is your luck that she happens to pass from this vale before you, and she need never suspect. Guard her well and cherish her; she is like money in the bank."

Nian Murrevil said: "Thank you, Sir Paul, for your provocative concepts; I am sure that they will linger with us. Next, is the eminent Professor Sounoutra Sukhail, a Grand Tantricist of the Antimates, and a Ninth Degree Putra. She will offer us excerpts from her paper on the mountain villages of Ladaque-Royale. I believe that she has something interesting to tell us regarding the human kites and the white wizards of the Pittispasian Cliffs, which as we all know limit the Central Massif of the Second Continent, where it abuts on the Groaning Ocean."

The florid man rose ponderously to his feet. "You are still referring to the planet Ladaque-Royale, Sagittarius FFC 32-DE-2930?"

Nian Murrevil said: "I do not have immediate access to the Final Functional Catalog, but I suspect that you have supplied the proper nomenclature, for which we owe you our gratitude."

"And Professor Sukhail is a Putra?"

"Exactly so; to the Ninth Degree. Now then, here is Professor Sukhail. Madame, you may now proceed with your address."

The Putra, a squat broad-faced woman with a shock of stiff auburn hair, spoke to the man in the front row. "You are correct in your designation, sir. Are you familiar with Ladaque-Royale?"

"I have studied the white wizards in depth! In fact, I can perform the Outremar Miracle, and I have gained access to the Tantric of the Lily Way."

"Aha!" said Sounoutra Sukhail. "I see that I cannot take liberties with the truth! But no matter; I will bridle my imagination and make do with a droning recitation of fact."

Sounoutra Soukhail need not have concerned herself; her unadorned facts were fascinating. She embellished them with photographs of the swooping gliding subjects, and she declared the abilities of the white wizards to be explained only in terms of thought transference. She looked down to the florid man in the front row. "Am I right in this belief, sir?"

"You are correct, in every respect," said the man solemnly. "I would endorse your remarks even were I not your husband."

Nian Murrevil stepped to the podium. "There will be a few moments delay while Professor Sukhail removes her equipment and exhibits."

For a period Luel and Perseia sat in silence. Then Perseia whispered to Luel: "When she spoke of thought transference and such things, I could not help but think of Jaro."

Luel considered the matter. "She takes the subject rather far afield. The 'Tantrickers' seem almost abnormal in their attributes, and the white wizards are remarkable, to say the least."

"I think Jaro might be something like that," said Perseia thoughtfully. "He has had these odd experiences, as you know. I believe they still trouble him."

"Nonsense!" said Luel shortly. "The Putra uses special terms! Jaro has never communed with these 'streams of transtemporal rays', nor does he do the seven Devores of Daily Duty."

"No, but he is undeniably what she calls a 'receptive'."

"I don't understand her terminology," Luel grumbled. "Still, I know what you are implying, and I do not totally disagree. Jaro, at the very least, is 'sensitive'."

Perseia nodded. "He is still troubled by the mystery of his origin — but that can't be the whole of it. There is surely something else gnawing at his mind, and I wish we could help him work it out."

Luel grunted. "He no longer gives us much serious consideration — especially with Evan Tarr on hand. His influence can't be altogether constructive."

Perseia pursed her lips doubtfully. "I don't think I would go quite that far. Evan Tarr has taught Jaro many practical skills."

"So it may be! But Evan Tarr does not share our social values; in fact, I consider him a vagabond living at the fringe of society, half predatory, totally lacking in moral convictions."

"Oh come now, Luel! You are throwing the baby out with the bath! Evan Tarr is a gentleman."

"For a gentleman he has a repertory of peculiar techniques. I consider him an avatar of violence, pain and death."

"Luel, you are talking nonsense. Evan Tarr obviously likes Jaro, and has devoted considerable effort to his practical education, where you and I would be helpless."

"So it may be," responded Luel tartly. "But next term Jaro is dropping classes in 'Non-semantic Poetry' and 'Symbology of Color' in order to find more time for his work at the space-port."

Perseia thought to change the subject. "Look yonder, just past the man in the blue cape."

Luel turned to look. "That is Dean Hutsenreiter, from the Institute. He's reading a paper on the Decoding and Translation of non-Gaean languages."

"That much I know; it's listed on the program. But who is that woman with him? Haven't we met her?"

Luel studied the tall woman in the striking purple and green garment. "That is his former wife — or maybe they are still legally bound, for all I know. She left him ten years ago, so I recall, and went off-world to her family estate."

Perseia covertly watched the dean and his handsome consort. "A curious situation."

"True. The dean is a curious fellow. He's a Clam Muffin but can't pay his creditors. I met him this morning by the newsstand; I nodded; he failed to recognize me. The woman was with him; perhaps he did not want to make tiresome explanations."

"Perhaps he was being a Clam Muffin."

"That, too, is conceivable."

"Strange. She's a striking woman. You can see where her daughter gets her looks."

" 'Daughter'? You mean that epicene little creature with the flat chest and long legs?"

Perseia smiled. "Have you seen her recently?"

"Not that I know of."

"When you do, look again."

Nian Murrevil stepped forward on the podium once again. "I am pleased to introduce our next speaker: a scholar of the most impeccable distinction: the Honorable Kyril Kasselbar."

Upon the podium appeared a tall man with a beak of a nose, fierce black eyes, a shock of white hair. Nian Murrevil spoke further, describing Kasselbar as a man whom he himself had revered almost since childhood; he was a linguist preeminent in the field, originally from Old Earth, now resident at the site of certain intriguing ruins, whose location he was not yet ready to reveal. Kasselbar stepped forward and described his efforts to translate the inscriptions on a set of eighty-five iridium alloy sheets, discovered in a shallow cave on a remote world of the Beyond. His recital was essentially a tale of incessant efforts to wring meaning from the incomprehensible markings. He told of the various artifices, techniques and tests he had used over the years — all to the same effect. As he finished, he glanced toward Nian Murrevil. "I suppose that by local standards I have earned for myself a very lowly and rather sordid tamsour." He spoke with a grim smile. "I have devoted many years to these inscriptions, and I have nothing whatever to show for my work: not even a pension from my university. They discharged me from their faculty over ten years ago. Still, I will scratch by, one way or another, and it may surprise you to learn that I have several new approaches I am desperately anxious to apply to the cursed inscriptions, and I can hardly wait to return to my office. Have I truly been cheated by the cosmos? I can not be sure.

"I might point out that sitting over yonder, as smug as ever and no doubt as erroneous as ever in his theories, sits Clarens Hutsenreiter. I worked with him once and even the laborers called him 'Careless Clarry', and every night they would take away his money at some gambling game. He mended his fortunes, so I am told, by assiduous and steamy proctosculation; also, he married a deluded heiress —"

Dean Hutsenreiter jumped to his feet and called: "Where is the monitor of ceremonies? How long will he tolerate this insane

rhodomontade? We hear the warblings of a madman; is there no sur-
cease? Monitor, do your duty, if you please!"

Nian Murrevil stepped forward and with great sangfroid induced
Kyril Kasselbar to relinquish the podium, though Kasselbar protested
that he wished to recount several other anecdotes of possible interest to the audience. As Nian Murrevil tried to lead him away, he cried
out: "Tomorrow you will hear a glib wash of footless generalities from
Careless Clarry. I had hoped to prepare you for his distortions. But
time seems to be at a premium. I can only suggest that you hold tight to
your purses when Clarry is near, and lend him no money. Alas! My lifetime has come and gone; my 'tamsour' — to use a local concept — will
be unremarkable, unless in my last golden years I decipher the plaques.
Then there will be glory indeed!" Kyril Kasselbar inclined his head
stiffly in response to the applause, and left the podium.

Perseia Fath notified Luel: "Dean Hutsenreiter gave only perfunctory applause. The lady with him was amused but casual."

Nian Murrevil reappeared. He made no reference to the linguist's
use of the word 'tamsour'. "Next you will hear the remarks of Professor
Luel Fath, from the Daniel Temianka Memorial Institute on Gallingale.
His topic, I am given to understand, is 'Aesthetic Symbology'."

Luel faced the audience. Usually he was comfortable in such situa-
tions, since he felt in command of his material and its interpretation.
But today, Dean Hutsenreiter sat in the audience, and worse, a Dean
Hutsenreiter boiling with fury.

Luel Fath wasted several seconds fussing with his papers, sipping
water, gazing around the audience — everywhere but toward Dean
Hutsenreiter. At last he cleared his throat and bravely commenced
to speak. He was annoyed to find that his voice sounded tremulous
and reedy. But there was no help for it. "My subject is vast. However,
it is coherent and universally consistent. I for one, would reject the
constraints Sir Paul Piatky would impose in the name of manageability.
After all, where is the harm in superabundance? If you are invited to a
banquet, you denounce not too much fine food, but its total absence.
Let us continue to celebrate the delectable crime of gluttony, with no
thought for the hollow-eyed vegetarian who glares at us so enviously.
Is it not plain then? Sir Paul must search for a new credo. 'Abundance',

'Plethora', 'Diversity' — these are the signposts pointing the way to a fine 'tamsour' — to use, or perhaps misuse, one of the peculiar local concepts. So much having been said, I take up my principal theme.

"Time is short and my scope is limitless; I will tell you only a few descriptive anecdotes. They will be both brief and to the point, since my subject, to be well and truly comprehended, requires an emotive perception of the symbols under consideration. I emphasize that every separate symbology — and there are many for even the most superficial appreciation, requires an enormous and extremely subtle study. I am sadly amused by persons who pretend to chic or avant-garde status by feigning enjoyment of the music of a culture different from their own since, of course, they instantly brand themselves poseurs.

"Still, it is possible to perceive the symbols without understanding their emotive force. There is, in fact, an intellectual satisfaction in simply recognizing the patterns. Often, I even think that I enjoy the music, though surely it is for the wrong reasons. Musical symbology must be imbibed with the mother's milk and the mother's voice and the sounds of the native homestead.

"My field is therefore doubly complex, since any study of a music must entail analysis of the society from which the symbology has sprung. The analyst will usually find fascinating correspondences which link the musical symbology with other aspects of the matrix. For instance —" Luel mentioned several societies, described their somatypes and typical costumes and played representative segments of each society's music. "You must listen closely. For each society I play first festive music, then music of circumstance, then funeral music. You will note interesting differences and interesting correspondences."

So went Luel's presentation, he finished with the statement: "Aesthetic symbology, naturally, is not confined to music, though it is perhaps most accessible for study. Other systems are more complex and more ambiguous. The concepts can be contradictory and extremely perplexing. I warn my students that if they hope to impose absolutes upon aesthetic symbology, he or she had better turn to a more malleable study."

Luel returned to his seat. Perseia assured him that his remarks had nicely engaged the interest of the audience, and that even Dean

Hutsenreiter had muttered what appeared to be grudging praise to his companion. "And now, if you are of a mind, I think I'd just as soon adjourn for a time."

" 'Adjourn'? You mean, 'leave the hall'?" Luel was surprised. "Whatever for? The session still has an hour to run."

Perseia grimaced. "So it does. I have heard too much weird talk of wizards and Jared's urgencies and moods and transferences. I think that I too am a borderline 'sensitive', or whatever such folk are called."

"Hmf," said Luel dubiously. "You leave, if you are uncomfortable. I would feel conspicuous if I left now."

Perseia subsided into her seat. "As soon as possible, then, let us leave this place. It gives me claustrophobia."

"Yes! As soon as we can decently make an exit."

Nian Murrevil introduced Dame Vaudres Neif, who discussed a topic which she called 'Sick Societies'. Before embarking upon her topic she also took time to refute Sir Paul for his proposals. "Like Luel Fath and no doubt many others among you, I deplore this sort of dreary pessimism. If we took Sir Paul seriously, we would terminate the conclave at this very instant and all go home, resign our places of honour and spend the rest of our lives in vegetarianism and apathy. I, for one, refuse to do so. Now then, some of you may be thinking that my topic, 'Sick Societies', is no less grim and portentous than that of Sir Paul's topic. Already my presentation has been called: 'Dame Neif's Brief Introduction to Eschatology'. This, of course, is a canard. For every 'sick society', dozens are healthy, where anything and everything may and probably does happen. Still, this is no reason for us to throw our hands in the air, click our heels and pull the coverlets over our heads." She frowned down at the florid man in the first row, who had jumped to his feet. "Well, sir?"

"You are addressing a literate audience. If your scholarship is as muddled as your metaphors, we are in for a painful afternoon." He bowed curtly and resumed his seat.

Dame Neif examined him for a moment, then said: "My topic is "Sick Societies' and you serve very nicely as a case study. Do you care to step up on the podium and submit to my examination?"

"I certainly do not care to do so," said the florid man stiffly. "Not unless first you step down here and submit to my own interesting examination."

Dame Neif proceeded with her topic, describing the characteristics of a sick society: its symptoms, maturity, decline and ultimate decay. "The superficial indications are by no means consistent. For instance, a static society need not be sick, if it is challenged by its environment. A society with disparities in privileges or wealth may be healthy if upward mobility is possible for persons who choose to work, train and exert themselves. The same society is sick if rewards and perquisites are given to drones and parasites who refuse to work. Isolated societies may well become strange and queer, but not necessarily sick. However, their risk is great, since they receive no corrective criticism. In which case, they are not aware of what might be a morbid degeneracy. Isolated societies are almost inevitably doomed to decay. Sacerdotal, religious or priest-dominated societies are like organisms with a cancer."

Dame Neif briefly developed her concepts, took some questions from the audience, then left the podium.

Nian Murrevil stepped forward, now wearing a conical hat of black velvet which accentuated the elegant pallor of his face.

"I wish to thank Dame Neif for her cogent remarks. I see that the time is verging toward the hour which we had stipulated for recess. We shall try to meet this schedule." A prim little smile appeared upon his face. "On Ushan we cite the dictum: 'All events must obey their imperatives.' So then — while the time is brief, only about six minutes, it will suffice for my own short presentation, which I was too modest to include upon the official calendar.

"The truth is, that in my own personal style, I too am a sociologist of a stature, so I believe, equivalent to your own; I make this assertion without embarrassment. Ah! you cry out in wonder, and you whisper back and forth: in which field does Sir Nian so quietly excel?" Nian Murrevil gave his head a sad shake. "It is a complex story, too detailed for the time available to us. Suffice it to say that my papers, embodying truly novel concepts, have never been published, and the propositions which should have gained universal currency have gone unheard, wasted, like so much trash. I have toiled like the fabulous Heracles against this shame; I have submitted my papers to every organ of intellectual broadcast I could discover. Unanimously they refused to cope with the novelty of my ideas. That is the gist of the story, and, though saddened, I will not complain. Instead, I have organized this conclave, where I can take a moment or so to express my views.

"This gathering includes the top skim of social anthropologists and related sciences from across the Gaean Reach; indeed, there is not one of you who has not published on Old Earth, and this of course is the touchstone of achievement. I congratulate you all, and, so saying, I request a brief period of your attention — now only three minutes until recess — to a truncated exposition of my views. And why should you not? You are here by my invitation and through the intricacy of my arrangements. When foundation funding was inadequate, I made up the shortfall from my private purse. So, as you see, I have committed a great deal of myself to the success of this conclave.

"But time is short, and I must make haste if I am so much as to adumbrate the scope of my thinking. I deal with the mystery of life, personality and individual destiny: concepts which are embodied in the idea of 'tamsour'.

"My thesis is that I have generated a cosmos by my own striving: a cosmos which draws its élan from my own life-energy, and uses my noble impulses to augment its characteristics. This cosmos, considering my natural attributes, should have been amiable and supportive; but, as you have heard, the opposite was the case and I met malice at every turn. Is it not strange and wonderful, that this cosmos of my own creation should in its arrogance draw itself up before me, mocking and sarcastic, to become my implacable tormentor?" Nian Murrevil leaned forward, face stern. "For a time I felt that we were evenly matched, but now the cosmos gains strength, and would reduce me to a paltry squeaking sub-thing, had I not found a means to blast the cosmos and its most precious darlings." Nian Murrevil glanced at a clock. "Ladies and gentlemen, the hour verges upon the time of recess, and the glorious, most dramatic tamsour ever conceived. I have outwitted the cosmos! I batter it, I destroy its precious things. I smash its ornaments; I knock it awry; I annihilate it! The time is — now!"

The central chandelier grew suddenly luminescent. In a fraction of a second, those who were looking up, saw it separate into flying

shards of colored glass with an eye-searing glare behind, which instan-
taneously expanded to fill the rotunda and explode the colored glass
of the great hemisphere into splinters, and so ended the conclave at
Dimplewater on the world Ushan, in a tamsour which would excite
murmurs of awe for centuries to come.

Chapter 4

1.

The big old house echoed with the sounds of emptiness. Jaro realized, with sorrow and guilt, that he had taken Luel and Perseia for granted, as if they would be with him forever. But now they were gone, along with all their kindness, good humor, and sheer decency and he could not bring them back.

Jaro sorrowfully but firmly put sentimentality aside and set about the dreary process of reorganizing his life. He immediately arranged for the removal of all the Faths' personal possessions; otherwise, everywhere he looked he would be reminded of their cheerful presence. Out the door went the Faths' clothes and most of their personal trinkets, though a few Jaro could not bring himself to abandon, and so, cursing his own flabbiness, put them into storage. In the end, Jaro was left with a house bare save for basic furniture, information files and his own possessions. Eventually he might put the house and the adjoining acreage up for sale. There was no need for an immediate decision, since the Faths, through careful investment, had left him without financial urgencies.

During the first two days after the news from Ushan, Jaro made a dozen attempts to reach Skirl at Mircla, her home on Nardessus Hill, without success. On the afternoon of the third day, a cool voice notified him that the bank had seized all of Clarens Hutsenreiter's assets and properties, and that the former occupants of Mircla House were no longer in residence. Jaro asked: "Where then can I find Skirl, Dean Hutsenreiter's daughter?"

There was a confused mutter, a delay and then Skirl's voice sounded in his ear. "Yes? Who is this?"

"Jaro. I've been trying to telephone you for two days."

Skirl said flatly: "I haven't been home; in fact, I've been busy at the bank."

"Their arrangements weren't satisfactory?"

"Not to me. Nor to them either, for that matter."

"Have you money?"

"Nothing to speak of. What about you?"

"No problems here. I'm relatively well-off. Where are you staying?"

"I don't know — yet."

"Wait there; I'll come pick you up."

After the slightest of hesitations, Skirl said: "Very well, I'll wait for you outside."

Jaro found her standing in the street beside a pair of travel cases. She wore a dark blue jacket and a short dark blue skirt; she stood erect, shoulders square, her face rather pale, taut and serious. She had the look of someone trying to solve a puzzle, and enlivened by an almost imperceptible excitement, or recklessness, or awareness of imminent — what could it be? Adventure? Exploration? Danger?

For an instant the two looked expressionlessly eye to eye, but there must have been an interchange of some sort, because the voice at the back of Jaro's head, which, since the news from Dimplewater, had been unwontedly quiet, suddenly groaned and sounded a hoarse babble of lament, and Jaro heaved a deep sigh. He loaded Skirl's cases into the runabout and they set off across Thanet, past the Institute and into Gwendolyne Road. Skirl said: "I've learned interesting things about my father. He was a financial genius. For every thousand sols worth of security he was able to borrow fifty thousand sols cash. The bankers are still puzzled. They came up with a solution. They want me to assume the indebtedness, from what they called a 'sense of honour'. When I laughed they became angry and told me to vacate the house at once. I'm just here now by accident, to pick up a few clothes."

Jaro attempted an off-hand manner. "You can stay with me as long as you like. There are no strings or obligations. I'll be happy for the company. You can have a guestroom or, if you like, the old main bedroom with a private bath."

"Whatever is convenient," said Skirl. "If the truth be known, I was on my way to your house. I planned to ask for a position as house-keeper."

"You are hired."

Skirl nodded indifferently; she had clearly taken as much for granted. "What are your plans?"

"They are simple. I want to quiet or drown or stifle or anything whatever the voice in my head."

Skirl turned him a frowning side glance. "The voice still troubles you — after all these years?"

"I thought that I had learned to ignore it, for some of the time at least. But it comes and goes."

Skirl winced. "Such a voice would drive me mad."

"I am not mad — yet. Now I'm free to do as I like and I want to turn it off."

"How can you do this?"

"I don't know for sure," said Jaro gloomily. "But I reason along these lines: when the Faths found me, I was in a state of shock — not to mention my physical condition. Apparently I had already been subjected to some sort of mental pressure, I think by my mother. From time to time, even now, I seem to feel her influence, and it makes me more uneasy than ever. In short, I must discover the facts of my early life."

"Hm. Do you hear the voice now?"

Jaro nodded. "It isn't happy. When I look at you, it groans and mumbles. If I were to touch you, it would try to kill me."

"Why?" Skirl asked in wonder.

"Jealousy."

Skirl laughed. "That is ridiculous! Our relationship is quite impersonal!"

"Of course."

Skirl darted Jaro another sidewise glance. "I will help you, as best I can."

Jaro nodded. Skirl seemed to expect no more. He said: "The voice may be my subconscious self, or a telepathic doppelganger, or the other half of a split personality: an alter ego, whom I have offended because of my dominance. It takes revenge in a spiteful fashion. If I conduct myself with anything other than absolutely straitlaced virtue, it will fill my head with sobs of pure misery."

Skirl said faintly: "This is a far stranger situation than any I had expected. It is a challenge, of sorts."

Jaro was puzzled. "I don't understand."

"No matter. What do you propose to do?"

"If I can discover the facts of my early life, I may quiet the voice, or expel it — whatever one does with such influences."

"I will help you," said Skirl with decision. "It will be, so to speak, the first case of my career."

"What career is that?"

"I have decided to become an effectuator*."

"I can use your help; no doubt as to that. Must I pay you?"

Skirl shook her head. "This will be practice. How do you want to proceed?"

"I want to go to the place where the Faths found me, and work backward from there."

"Where is this place?"

"I don't know. The Faths would not tell me. They said that my education came first. When I tried to argue, they hid all the records."

"That seems a bit excessive."

"Yes, perhaps. But we shouldn't have much trouble finding the records."

"I shouldn't think so."

Jaro and Skirl arrived at Merrihew. Skirl decided to use the main bedroom, with its private bath. She looked around the old house without enthusiasm; it seemed austere and graceless. Jaro explained that he had not been expecting company and had discarded everything which had given the house its previous character. He agreed that he had acted by reflex, or a convulsive reaction against an emotional overload. In the long run it would make little difference, since he might well sell, if someone made him a reasonable offer. Skirl advised him not to be too hasty, but to do some research on land values.

---

* Effectuator: a private investigator, or agent; someone who is paid to achieve some sort of deed, or produce a desired effect. Some effectuators are persons of great skill, ingenuity and high principle; others cannot be distinguished from ordinary criminals, and have given the trade a dubious reputation.

"That's already been done," said Jaro. "A little while ago a land agent from Thanet made Luel an offer of twenty-two thousand sols*. Luel said that he thought the offer was a bit low, but when he looked into land prices, he found twenty-two thousand was close to an average price, providing that the house was valued at next to nothing which may or may not be realistic, depending upon the taste of the ultimate buyer."

"It's a bit of an old barn," said Skirl. "If I owned the property, I'd tear it down and build a pretty little cottage back off the road, near the forest."

On the following day Jaro took Skirl to the spaceport and pointed out the machine shop. "I've been working here part time with a man who calls himself Evan Tarr, though that's not his name. Still, it's none of my affair. He is something of a vagabond and I think that Perseia might have been fascinated by him — quite innocently, of course, and only just enough to irritate Luel. He is the only friend I have in the Reach. Not counting you, of course."

Skirl laughed uncertainly. "What an odd thing to say! Why not count me?"

Jaro was embarrassed. "I was afraid that you would sneer, and point out that you were a Clam Muffin; that I was nothing but a wanderling, with the status of an experimental client."

Skirl laughed. "Jaro! I do so like it when you pretend to be modest! Remember: I have no friends at all — not counting you, of course."

Jaro had nothing to say. After a moment he reached out and ruffled her short thick dark hair, and put it into a tangle. Skirl ducked out of reach and used both hands to bring her hair back into a semblance of order. Jaro saw that she could barely restrain a grin. It might have been the first time in her life that anyone had dared such indignities upon her person.

They stopped to admire a large space yacht, of superlative power

---

* Sol: Unit of Currency across the Gaean Reach, traditionally valued at the worth of an hour of unskilled labor. The value fluctuated from place to place, but in general retained its equivalence. At Thanet, for instance, a construction laborer might easily be hired for eight sols for an eight-hour workday.

and elegance. "That's the *Pharsang*, a Falco Glitterway, built at the Madel Shipyards on Rodino. Tarr and I have been installing new equipment in the pilothouse."

Skirl gave him a glance of puzzled appraisal. "How long have you worked here?"

"About three years. The Faths thought I was wasting my time, especially when it cut into my schedule at the Institute."

"You must have had good reasons."

"I thought they were good. I admired Evan Tarr and wanted to learn what he could teach me."

"And you've done so?"

Jaro gave a sour laugh. "He surprises me every day. He is competent, in a dozen different directions. Also, I wanted money which had not derived from the Faths, and so put me under their control. Luel sensed some of this, and of course his feelings were hurt, since he and Perseia had planned an academic career for me. Evan Tarr was a bad influence. Luel decided to take steps. With all his diligence he traced Tarr's background and found that his name was probably 'Dain Maihac'. He also found that the IPCC considered both Evan Tarr and Dain Maihac innocent of any wrongdoing, to Luel's disappointment, so I am sure. He still suspected Tarr of trying to dodge creditors or avoid an importunate wife. It was transparently reasonable, he argued, that when persons used false names, they are concealing themselves from someone. He even quoted Baron Bodissey: 'Honest folk do not wear masks when they enter a bank'. Luel was pleased with the quotation, and thought that no more need be said on the subject."

"Hmf," said Skirl. "Luel sounds a bit stuffy."

Jaro sighed. "Evan Tarr stirred up his sense of inadequacy."

"Where is Evan Tarr now?"

"On the *Pharsang*. It's up for sale and the owner is instructing Tarr in regard to repairs."

"Does Tarr know of the voices in your head?"

"No. I've never wanted him to think I was crazy."

"Hm. Interesting. I don't think you are crazy."

"Well then! What, for a fact, do you think of me?"

Skirl evaded the question. "Can we go aboard the *Pharsang*?"

"Not today, with Norby Mildoon aboard, wiping up specks of dust with his handkerchief. He's never taken the vessel aloft; can you believe it?"

Skirl looked over the space yacht. "It's beautiful — more than beautiful. It's the symbol of flight, and freedom of passage to all the far places."

Jaro said gloomily: "Don't covet it; you can break your heart wanting a ship like that. It's not just a rich man's toy — which this one happens to be. It's large enough to carry freight, or passengers, but it's still agile enough to be put down on a small field or even on a body of water."

"How much does such a ship cost?"

"It depends upon interior finish. This one should go for about two hundred thousand, since it's equipped with standard fittings, nothing too lavish."

The two turned away toward the machine shop.

"My own tastes are more modest," said Jaro. "I'd like to find a small disreputable freighter, broken and more or less abandoned at the back of a big yard, buy it cheap and rebuild it to proper standards, taking my time, and putting Tarr to work if he'd condescend, and then go out carrying cargoes of opportunity through the back-worlds where the scheduled packets don't touch. But, naturally, only after I had straightened myself out, and could call myself 'sane' without looking over my shoulder."

"How much would that kind of freighter cost?"

Jaro shrugged. "Anywhere between ten and thirty or forty thousand sols. Then — renew and rebuild, another ten to twenty thousand. The whole package: well under a hundred thousand."

Skirl gave a sad laugh. "My mother misbehaved badly at Castle Klankxby on Marmaude. She paid dearly for the lapse. She lost her Purple; she was excised from six of the seven temples and disinherited by my grandfather of a million sols. She sent me back to Gallingale and performed even worse than before. Instead of inheriting at least a million sols, I am totally forgotten at Castle Klankxby. Everything considered, this is best. I never liked either my father nor my mother, nor any of my family. I have become cynical and ruthless; in short, I will be a good effectuator, and earn a fortune. If you come under my command, you will be assigned cases too vulgar or ordinary to interest me; you will deal with low-caste machinators, double-diseasers, and other dubious types. You will be paid adequately — but I had forgotten; you won't need the job, since the Faths left you well-off."

"Comfortably so, but nothing lavish. I can't buy any space yachts with an income of three hundred sols a month. In a year I can save two thousand sols. In ten years I'd have something over twenty thousand sols: enough to get started on a low-status hulk."

"Suppose you sold the house?"

"Then I'd have no place to live and I could save only a hundred sols a month, depending upon my standard of living, and whether I joined the Scythians or the Squared Circles."

"Small chance of that. How much would you get for the house?"

Jaro considered. "Luel received an offer a few months ago, from a broker named Norby Mildoon. It must be the same man who owns the *Pharsang*. Mildoon offered Luel twenty-two thousand sols, as I recall."

"What of the investments? Can you realize anything on them?"

Jaro laughed. "The Faths locked their investments into a trust account which I can't liquidate until I am fifty years old."

"It seems as if the Faths knew you well."

"What they did not know they suspected. Look yonder; see that tall dark-haired man in the green jacket! That is Evan Tarr."

Skirl stared. "He is — startling!"

"He has scars elsewhere which are just as bad. He won't talk about them. After a few minutes you'll stop noticing. But it is better to know what to expect before you meet him."

Evan Tarr sat at a table, working to repair a small mechanism. Skirl watched him in fascination and whispered to Jaro: "Why doesn't he have his face restored? Does he enjoy shocking people?"

"Luel had the same idea," said Jaro, rather shortly. "He implied that Tarr was either psychotic, or an exhibitionist. I had no sensible answer, so the next day I asked Evan Tarr. He seemed surprised that anyone should wonder. He said that for the most part he never thought of the scars, and that some day he would have them removed. I asked why he waited. He said that it was not all so simple, and that he would tell me the story someday when we had time. Meanwhile the scars were a source of strength for him."

"Those are strange remarks!"

"That is my whole life," said Jaro. "A mosaic of mysteries, strange remarks, sinister shapes against the sunset, tragic voices —"

"Nevertheless, a brilliant young effectuator has taken up your case, and at last you may rest easy."

"The brilliant young effectuator has attracted Evan Tarr's attention, so now you will meet him. One last word: don't mention the name 'Maihac'; he doesn't know I know."

Skirl nodded. "I will be discreet."

Evan Tarr rose to his feet as they approached, the disconnected elements of a smile further contorting the contours of his face. Jaro introduced Skirl with formality, as a Clam Muffin, the bereaved daughter of Dean Hutsenreiter, and a practising effectuator at the start of her career. She had set up temporary offices in Merrihew, since there was more than enough room for them both.

Evan Tarr seemed impressed; he looked at Skirl's hands and complimented her: "These are the hands of a practical person, he said, neither small nor delicate, but deft and competent: hands which could be trusted with tools or weapons or the navigation of a sailboat." Jaro could see that she was pleased by the remark. Tarr went on to say that if his first impressions were to be trusted, Skirl would do well in her future career. Jaro thought that Skirl seemed irrationally pleased by what might have passed for a conventional compliment.

Evan Tarr put aside his work for the day. The three dined in a modest tavern in the woods, where folk from Thanet came to spend a quiet evening.

At first Evan Tarr had little to say, then gradually he seemed to relax. He admitted that for many years he had lived the life of a vagabond, then had become the master of a small freighter plying remote ports of far worlds, carrying cargoes and passengers as circumstance dictated. "As I think of it now, it was a life of constant change, exotic adventure, and — from time to time — danger."

Skirl asked: "Danger enough to put the scars on your face?"

"Yes," said Evan Tarr. "That would be a fair judgment."

Skirl gave her head a marvelling shake. "Why did you come to Thanet? Life here must seem very dull."

Evan Tarr considered a moment. "I am at Thanet, because I have to be somewhere. At any place in the Gaean Reach where I happened to be, someone might put the same question to me. As for life here being dull, not so. May I become a bit abstract, or philosophical?"

"Within limits," said Jaro. "Just use words we can understand."

"Of course! How could it be otherwise? I am the vagabond; you two have had expensive educations at the Daniel Temianka Memorial Institute of Pantology."

"True," said Jaro. "We cannot deny this."

Tarr went on to describe what he termed "— the entertainment provided by Fate and its vagaries. Each instant is a surprise! Drama is everywhere — sometimes large, sometimes small, sometimes maddeningly ambiguous. Trivial matters can become a source of suspense." Tarr looked around the room for an example, and indicated the next table, which was occupied by a fat gentleman and a tall, pale, languorously beautiful woman. With long red plumes they guided bubbles of intoxicating gas from an expressor at the center of the table to their faces. The gentleman sniffed and snapped at the bubbles; the woman wielded her long red plume in a manner so charmingly degagé as to invite admiration. Tarr first propounded as his drama a contest as to which would inhale the most and biggest bubbles in a minute. The gentleman emerged victorious from the contest. Tarr then proposed a second drama: would the gentleman succeed in seducing the woman before the night was over? Skirl, who had shown little interest in the first contest, looked over her shoulder. "No," she said. "Definitely not."

"You are strangely certain," said Jaro.

"I had not looked at them carefully before. I see now that the fat man is Mr. Tantroy, the banker who just now evicted me from Mircla. The woman's name is Hortense; she is my father's old mistress."

"And so?"

Skirl shrugged. "Hortense is a tireless climber, although she is only a 'Thespian', of the meanest sort. She has been trying to 'roll herself upstairs' — as the parlance goes. But she'll have no luck with Mr. Tantroy, even though he is a Scythian."

"Hm," said Jaro. "Scythians are notoriously gallant."

"He notoriously suffers from impotence. Whatever he wants with Hortense, it is not the plunder of her long marmoreal body."

"Just so," said Evan Tarr. "It all goes to illustrate my point. There is drama everywhere!"

Tarr was now completely at ease, thought Jaro. He need not have feared for Skirl's adverse opinion. She seemed tired, pensive, but quite relaxed, as if she were in the company of persons she totally trusted. Jaro thought that she looked both older and younger than her years. Of one thing he was certain: if not on Evan Tarr, she was making a strongly favorable impression upon himself. He winced at the thought of the keening watchdog at the back of his mind. For the moment it lay quiescent as if asleep, or huddled in the dark. Jaro knew that the stillness was transitory; should he touch Skirl, stroke her hair or kiss her, he would provoke a wild surge of howling misery, so that he might be prompted to — well, no, thought Jaro, stealing a glance toward Mr. Tantroy; that wasn't really what he had in mind. The single solution remained: he must rid himself of his incubus.

Jaro looked at Skirl. She was smiling toward a place halfway between himself and Evan Tarr. Jaro sighed. Perhaps the admonitions of the dreary voice were just as well; for the moment he wanted no more complications in his life than those with which he already must cope. On the other hand, came the counter-argument, that — all taken with all — the complication represented by Skirl would be something other than irksome.

Upon leaving the tavern Evan Tarr bade them goodnight and went to his own lodgings. Jaro and Skirl returned to Merrihew, which seemed more graceless and uninviting than ever. The two went rather gingerly to sit in the drawing room, where they drank tea and regarded each other sidelong. Finally Skirl said: "I'm tired, and I think I'll go to my room."

"We'll talk more in the morning," said Jaro.

But instead of rising to her feet and leaving the room, Skirl relaxed into her chair and sat watching the flames in the fireplace. She said musingly: "I wonder how Evan Tarr came by his scars."

Jaro thought back over what he knew of the inscrutable vagabond. He finally admitted that Tarr had never explained the scars in detail, other than to say that they represented annual counters, like the growth rings in tree trunks.

"How did you discover that his name was not 'Evan Tarr'?"

Jaro smiled in bitter reminiscence. "It was not I who did the discovering. Luel Fath was driven by curiosity and distrust and perhaps a bit of jealousy. His self-esteem was based not on membership in the Clam Muffins, but upon pride in his eclectic intellect, and his belief that the aesthetic philosopher was the most majestic of all human beings. Evan Tarr's casual competences raised doubts in his mind as to who was truly the better man, and Luel subconsciously wondered whether it might not be Evan Tarr."

Skirl appraised him curiously. "And you agreed?"

Jaro shook his head. "I made no judgments then, and I don't now."

"It's not a fair question to begin with," said Skirl. "Different people are at their best in different circumstances."

True," said Jaro. "If it came to basic courage, plain and simple, I think Luel Fath would show very well, intellectual or not. And I can't fault him for the same curiosity I feel toward Evan Tarr — though for different reasons."

"I'm curious too," said Skirl. "What did Luel do?"

"Nothing disgraceful. When I first began working at the spaceport Perseia thought it would be nice to invite Evan Tarr in for supper, and she did so. He was punctual, properly dressed and decently attentive to Luel's opinions.

"Then began the business of the fish knife." Jaro explained it in as much detail as he could remember. During the first course, Perseia commented upon Tarr's use of the fish knife. "Your grip is a variant of an old-fashioned style of etiquette rather rare, nowadays."

Tarr was surprised by the news, since he had assumed his usage to be standard. Perseia assured him that his table manners were neither odd nor vulgar. "When you dine with social anthropologists, you must expect to find strange topics creeping into the conversation."

Luel explained to him that Perseia had recently read a research paper on the topic, and now she watched everyone eat with an embarrassing intensity. Perseia denied that she was quite so keen, but promised to be less analytical during the rest of the meal.

Tarr only laughed. "My father was school master in the backlands of Paghorn, which is a place of no significance and you will never hear of it again. There were five children and my mother was determined to raise us as ladies and gentlemen, using a book called 'Godfroy's Guide to Delicate Manners'. At every meal we were faced with a full range of implements, while the local folk, used only what they called 'scoops', 'nuppers' and their fingers. As I think back, they were really a rather loutish folk."

Perseia asked: "What happened to your brothers and sisters?"

Tarr said he did not know, that he was the black sheep of the family and had left home early.

After he had gone Perseia said she thought that Evan Tarr seemed very nice, and certainly a gentleman, black sheep or not. Luel remained dour. In his opinion Tarr was undoubtedly a vagabond, if not worse, no matter how nicely he gripped his fish knife. Perseia laughed. Jaro said nothing, since Luel had improperly used his own fish knife, and there the matter rested.

Two months later Luel casually mentioned that Tarr seemed to be using a false name. Jaro had already noticed that Tarr had engraved the initials 'D. M.' on some of his tools. Perseia asked how Luel could be so certain; he said he had sent off for appropriate reference works; Paghorn was otherwise known as Leo KJL 334 - III, and was indeed a wild rough world, of many contrasts, sparsely inhabited by the Juba: a stolid country folk who derived their livelihood from farming and the sea. They were descended from a colony of Flinchtree Nihilists, who abominated institutions of any kind, and who developed a society without towns, villages, schools, temples, offices, or civic organizations with any kind of permanent staff. Gangora was their cooperative trading post, and here an ideal Parnassian named Vervan Maihac founded his Academy for the Training of Young Gentlemen and Young Ladies in the Liberal Arts. By some miracle the academy survived; Vervan Maihac was succeeded by his son Fionn, who met a cultured and idealistic young woman named Myrilla Maubry at the Teacher's College and brought her back to Paghorn. Their first four children were girls. The Gangora directory listed a fifth child, a son Dain, who disappeared from the directory during his sixteenth year; presumably he had gone off-world. The names 'Tarr' or 'Evan Tarr' appeared nowhere in Paghorn records. The names

'Dain Maihac' and 'Evan Tarr' were both absent from IPCC files of known malefactors.*

Luel summed the matter up. "It looks to me as if Dain Maihac, after leaving an extremely genteel home, might have over-compensated, to become a vagabond who now thinks it best to use the name 'Evan Tarr'."

"Yes," said Perseia. "That is a sensible judgment."

Luel looked at her with sandy eyebrows raised. "Is that all you can say?"

Perseia considered. "He seems to demonstrate the best aspects of both worlds, which is surely no mean accomplishment."

Luel turned away, unable to fit words to his feelings and no more was said, though Evan Tarr was not again invited to Merrihew.

Skirl gave the matter thought. "I incline to Perseia's theories, for the most part."

"Oh? And what part remains?"

Skirl hunched her shoulders. "I don't understand his moods. This makes me uneasy."

"Hm," said Jaro. "And you understand all my moods?"

"Of course." She darted him a quick glance. "Naturally."

Jaro sighed, shrugged and, defeated, turned to look into the fire. "He's a person I respect."

Skirl jumped to her feet with sudden energy. "He is impervious and I don't think he likes me!"

"Of course he likes you!" declared Jaro in astonishment. "How could anyone not like you?"

"Quite easily, I think."

"Why should Evan Tarr not like you?"

Skirl shrugged. "He knows that I don't believe much of what he tells us. Still, he has a right to his secrets, and I can't practice being an

---

* It may be noted here that the researches performed by Luel Fath were neither complicated nor unusual; he need look only in an index, make selections among the hundreds of references available to him, then wait, for at most a month. The information was at the disposal of anyone with access to a library. The IPCC (Interworld Police Coordination Company) were required to maintain records at all times open to public scrutiny. Luel, in short, had consulted the public record.

effectuator upon everyone I meet. And now, I'm really off to bed." She marched from the room, slight figure erect, shoulders square, neck stiff. Jaro was reminded of his first glimpse of the proud Skirlet Hutsenreiter at the elementary school.

At the door Skirl paused and spoke over her shoulder. "Tomorrow I begin my career. Before long the mystery will be resolved and the sad voice will once more be at peace with itself."

"I don't want it at peace! I want it gone, so that I can have some privacy!"

"I will take the matter in hand," said Skirl over her shoulder.

"The sooner the better," Jaro muttered and presently took himself to bed.

2.

In the morning Jaro and Skirl set about solving the mystery of Jaro's past. "The first step is to identify the place where they found me," said Jaro. "The information should be in their journals, but I can't find it."

"Where are these journals?"

"In the case yonder."

The two investigated the journals, workbooks and reports relevant to the period during which the Faths had come upon Jaro. It soon became clear that the Faths had meticulously screened all this material for any mention of the place in question. Careful search revealed nothing. What the Faths could not excise from their records, they had transcribed into a set of incomprehensible numerals. Skirl became indignant at what she considered a cold-blooded attempt to thwart Jaro. "There is something ruthless here, and rather sly. The Faths might have been gentle and mild, but this is not a pretty look into their minds."

Jaro was more temperate. "What you find here is not so much harshness or cruelty but Luel's meticulous precision. Luel could not undertake a job and do it half-way, and, remember, they worked in what they considered my best interests."

"They wanted you to gain a degree in philosophy and be like themselves."

Jaro laughed sadly. "They feared that I would take the bit into my teeth and set off on a wild quest, despite their best advice. They have been proved right."

The morning passed, and nowhere could be found a mention of the Wyching Hills. Jaro and Skirl lunched on cucumbers, ragout, bread, wine and olives; then Skirl went off to her old home Mircla on Nardessus Hill, where she hoped to salvage a few more of the family's personal effects, and Jaro was left to sit in the dim old drawing room, to gaze into the fire. No question, he thought, but what he had entered a new phase of existence, governed by new forces and the inclinations of different people — which, for all practical purposes, meant Skirl. He thought about her as impersonally as he could, but was still roused to an excitement which must be curbed before the voice started to whimper and tell of its own frustrations. Jaro sighed and went to continue his scrutiny of odd notes and memoranda.

The day wore on. Skirl returned, in a bad mood. Over dinner she told of her misadventures. She had secured access to Mircla only with difficulty, and had been denied each of her requests. She wanted no more to do with the past. She would never go back to Mircla, even if she were begged to on bended knees. She was considering that she might resign her life membership in the Clam Muffins. She sat beside Jaro, brooding into the fire, then, abruptly, took herself off to bed.

In the morning the two continued their examination of files, letters, documents, schedules and expense accounts: to no avail. It was as if Luel had foreseen the search and had made a game of his deletions. It was a frustrating exercise, which the two completed shortly after noon. At this time Jaro was not thinking kindly thoughts about either Luel or Perseia.

Almost as if on cue, the Faths' legal counsel, Wolber Imbald, visited Jaro at Merrihew. Imbald was middle-aged, portly, with a sleek ruff of white hair, small black eyes and a snub nose in a round pink cheerful face; his garments were expensive if untidy; he belonged to the Titularies and the Brummagem Club, so that his social level was somewhat higher than that of the Faths, though it still fell short of that represented by the Squared Circles, much less the Scythians or the Clam Muffins. Jaro ushered him into the Merrihew drawing-room. Skirl remained out of sight in the kitchen.

Wolber Imbald spoke in tones of mock aggrievedness. "I've been waiting for you to call on me."

"Sorry," said Jaro. "I've been busy sorting things out. As you can imagine, I've been busy."

"Yes, of course." Imbald looked around the bleak drawingroom. "As you must know, the Faths bequeathed everything to you, without qualification, and you are left, if I may say so, relatively well-off."

Jaro nodded. "I know, and I am properly grateful—though I would much rather have them back."

"They were fine people," Imbald agreed. Again he glanced around the room, taking note of its bleak condition. "Are you planning to sell?"

Jaro shrugged. "I have no definite plans. It depends upon what offers I hear. I'm not in any hurry."

Imbald pursed his lips judiciously. "Just so. If you have any questions, don't hesitate to call on me. But that is not why I am here. Two months ago the Faths put a letter and a parcel into my custody. I will give you the letter now." Wolber Imbald reached into his pocket and brought out a long brown envelope which he handed to Jaro. "I do not know the contents of this letter. I assume that it pertains to the parcel."

Jaro read the letter:

"Dear Jaro: This is written as a hedge against a set of highly unlikely circumstances: which is to say, the sudden death of both of us. If you read this letter—the Fates forfend!—it means that these unlikely and sorrowful circumstances have come to pass, and we therefore mourn (along with you, so we hope) the passing of our lives. A strange thought, as I sit here writing this! But, as you know, we try to be both logical and providential. It is foolish to leave anything to chance, when this element can be eliminated. So—if you read this—the event we all deplore has occurred, and we are dead! Nor, on a less awful scale, will you have finished your curriculum at the Institute. We recognize that you are susceptible to impulses which might propel you out upon a wild crusade in search of your origins, before you take your degree. We believe this to be inadvisable, and hope to make a rational sequence of events easier and hence preferable to you.

Be assured! we sympathize with your anguish, and we are reluctant to be the agents of your frustration, but we are convinced that it is in your best interests to gain that education which will establish for you a solid and respected place in society. It is an excellent thing to have earned a degree at the Institute!

So, to this end, we have placed the information which is yours by right in a trust account, which will be opened to you the day after you are graduated from the Institute with representative honors.

Naturally we hope that you will never read this letter. On the day following your matriculation you will be mystified by the little ceremony we make of its burning.

Your loving foster parents,
Luel and Perseia

Jaro looked at the lawyer. "I do not intend to continue at the Institute."

"Then you will never receive the parcel placed in the trust account."

"Is there no way to bypass these provisions? Neither Luel nor Perseia fully understood the urgency which presses on me."

The lawyer inspected him curiously. "If I may ask a personal question: why do you insist upon such haste? Why not obey the wishes of your foster parents? They seem both reasonable and far-sighted — especially since you are clearly as headstrong as they had feared?"

Jaro heaved a sad sigh. "It is something I cannot explain to you."

"Try me. After all, I am human, though a lawyer."

"You would not take me seriously. You would probably decide that I was unbalanced."

"Still, why not take the chance?"

Jaro shrugged. "As you like. It can do no harm. I could not confide in the Faths; when I tried, their response was to call in the psychiatrists."

"And what was their verdict?"

"They found names and classifications, but they understood

nothing and solved nothing and did in the end nothing. For a very good reason."

"And what is the reason?"

Jaro hesitated. "I won't use the word 'real', because I can't demonstrate anything. All I can do is explain how I am affected."

"Very well; explain your problems."

"The Faths called them 'hallucinations', though Perseia once or twice speculated about 'thought-transference'. Either way, they happen at night. A mood of cold sadness comes over me; if I am asleep, I wake up to this mood. It is like a mixture of grief and longing and frustration."

"Isn't that rather like a nightmare?"

Jaro made an impatient gesture. "No. There is no distortion, even though I feel as if another person were imprisoned in a dark chamber lost somewhere at the back of my mind."

"There is always the possibility of a so-called 'double personality'."

"I can only report what I feel, and I do not consider myself a 'double personality', nor am I unbalanced. The moods are not so bad now; I have learned to control them, but when I was young and these moods came upon me, my mind was a frightening place, dark and lonely, where awful things occur. Sometimes a voice in the distance cried out for help. I thought to recognize my own voice."

The lawyer winced. "If you are not crazy, you have every right to be so. But you are clearly quite sensible. I think that you should be able to accept the Faths' position. In any case, another —"

A knock sounded at the front door; Jaro admitted Evan Tarr, whom he introduced to Wolber Imbald, and tersely explained Imbald's visit. "He does not think I am crazy, but he won't give me the parcel."

Imbald beamed a jovial smile from face to face around the group. "Of course I don't think you are crazy. Still, another attempt at therapy is preferable to a wild excursion across the Reach in search of voices which originate inside your own brain."

Evan Tarr said: "You seem to be telling us that if the voices are inside Jaro's head, he can search for them as easily here, in this room, than on some nameless asteroid a thousand light-years away."

"Just so!" declared Imbald enthusiastically. "And meanwhile, he can pursue his studies at the Institute."

"The question would become moot if I had the information which you are withholding from me."

"The Faths are withholding the information," said Imbald politely. "Their motives, however, are benign."

Tarr smiled his crooked smile. "The Faths are dead. Alive, they were decent people, but what of that? Is decency everything in life?"

Imbald spoke ponderously: "The short answer is 'yes'. Codified decency is law."

"The Faths carried decency too far," said Jaro. "They planned my life; they wanted me to take a secure chair at a reputable academy with full tenure and membership in the faculty club."

"Nothing wrong with that," said Wolber Imbald bluffly. "A person could do far worse. The Institute is a reputable establishment."

Evan Tarr said thoughtfully: "The Institute is a fancy aviary for tame birds. No one flies very far afield, and the biggest bird sits on the highest perch. Everyone below must keep a wary eye cocked upward."

Wolber Imbald rose to his feet. "I have nothing more to say. I advise you to return to your studies at the Institute." He bowed politely and took his leave.

After a moment Tarr asked Jaro: "So what do you think you will do?"

"My program runs in a circle. I want to quiet the voice in my head. That means I must learn about my early life. I have only a few memories. If I go to where the Faths found me, I may be able to trace my life backward to my mother and my father. I don't know where this place is, and if I did know, then I would need to sell the house in order to go there. If I am forced to attend the Institute, I will want to live in the house — which I don't want to do." Jaro took some papers off the table and looked at them. "These are transcripts of what I told the psychiatrists under hypnosis. It is not very much. I remembered an old house built of yellow clapboard, on a strip of swampy ground between a growth of tall cane grass and a river. I remember the figure of a man silhouetted against the sunset sky. My mother saw it also. It seems that I used the name 'Asrubal', though I don't remember doing so. My mother became frightened; I can never see her face, but she was warm and loving. Under hypnosis I heard her voice, which again I don't remember." Jaro glanced at the papers. "She said: 'Don't forget! You must never forget! I can do no more for you, and now, like your father, I must die. But someday come back here, find what I have given you and destroy Asrubal! My poor little Jaro, with so much sorrow to undergo!' The psychiatrists note that I was uttering disjointed phrases; that they have rendered a paraphrase. I remember darkness, a boat, wind, cold water, and I remember swimming. Then nothing more until I became conscious in the hospital, with the Faths looking down at me. But what hospital, at what town, on what world? The Faths gave the information to Wolber Imbald, and he won't give it to me."

Evan Tarr mused a moment. "The information should not be too hard to access. If I took Wolber Imbald into the woods and started pulling off his toe nails, he would shower us with parcels of every sort." Noticing Skirl's wry expression, Evan Tarr laughed. "But it need not come to that."

Jaro asked: "There is another way, a bit less noisy?"

"Yes, I think so, and we need not disturb the lawyer. Do you remember how I first met Perseia?"

"You donated some exotic musical instruments to her department museum."

Evan Tarr nodded. "It was an artifice, of course, and it succeeded. I became friendly with the Faths."

Jaro was surprised. "But why would you want to do that?"

Evan Tarr dismissed the matter with a wave of the hand. "Perhaps I should not have mentioned it. In any case, Perseia took me to the library and showed me her collection of unconventional musics. There is no way she could have altered the records at the Music Department library."

Half an hour later Evan Tarr, Jaro and Skirl were examining the archives at the Institute Music Library, taking note of the specific musics recorded during the year they had found Jaro. The records were plain. During the designated interval, the Faths had roamed the Wildenberry Steppe on the world Kammerwelt, near the village Stronk, west of the Wyching Hills.

"So much for that," said Jaro. "Now, all I need is money."

"Don't look at me," said Skirl. "I have nothing except for what you are paying me, which so far has been very little, in fact nothing."

Jaro said gloomily, "If I must, I will sell the house — if I can get a proper price. Perhaps I'll let Norby Mildoon know that I might be interested in hearing an offer."

Skirl frowned. "Norby Mildoon? Isn't he the Zonker who owns the big space yacht?"

"He doesn't truly own it," said Jaro. "He's only making payments on the mortgage."

"He'll offer you cheese parings if he thinks you are anxious to sell."

Jaro said confidently: "I won't act anxious; I'll act as if I have plenty of money and selling the house means nothing."

"He may offer you even less."

Jaro reported on his encounter with Norby Mildoon later in the day. "I went into his office; I was quite casual, and he kept me waiting twenty minutes. I had started out the door, when his secretary called me back. She had already explained my business to him, so that he wasted no time in doodling with the price. He looked into a notebook, told me that the Association valuation upon the property was sixteen thousand seven hundred and thirty-three sols. I asked if that was for the house or the property? He said both, and that real estate values were flat. So I said good afternoon and left."

"You did quite correctly," said Skirl. "Tomorrow we will organize our intellects and contrive a set of profitable enterprises which will quickly and easily earn us a great deal of money."

"That is a very good idea," said Jaro. "More than ever I am glad that I hired you."

"So much is settled then," said Skirl. "Let's look up 'Kammerwelt' in the 'Handbook'."

Jaro found a copy of *Handbook to the Planets*, and turned to the entry describing 'Kammerwelt', fourth world in the entourage of Robert Palmer's Star, away and out toward the edge of the galaxy. The entry was brief but informative.

Robert Palmer's Star drifted slowly through a sector known as 'the Dragon's Maw': a region notable for its splendid astronomical spectacles. Robert Palmer's Star, no exception, shone brilliant and white, its corona flaring with films of blue, red and green color. A dozen planets danced attendance, like children careening about a maypole, but only

Kammerwelt knew that narrow range of conditions tolerant to human existence.

The Faths' old information repository provided further information; text, graphs and pictures appeared on the screen. Kammerwelt was described as a world with Earth-normal characteristics, with a flora and fauna of Style ABA-CAA* compatibility. With the exception of the enormous flying insects of the Goleta and the Velvinor departments, and the grass jungles of the Latvold, the most remarkable examples of local flora and fauna were confined to the Concordia and Misericordia Continental Preserves. Elsewhere the environment was more or less benign. In recent years, however, Kammerwelt's population had been declining, so that a number of small outlying communities had been abandoned.

Jaro and Skirl studied maps of Kammerwelt. From the town Stronk a road led north, with the Wyching Hills to the west and the Wildenberry Steppe to the east.

Jaro touched a point on the road with his finger. "There you see it — the spot where the Faths found me. How did I get there? I have a feeling I came over the Wyching Hills. I can't be sure, but when I think of low mustard-yellow hills with the river snaking across the landscape behind me, I feel something like déjà vu."

"Poor little boy!" said Skirl feelingly.

Jaro uttered a short self-conscious laugh. "It could have been worse. Now nothing is needed but money enough to take me —"

"And me."

"— and you to Kammerwelt."

On the following morning, while Skirl had gone off to transact business of her own, Norby Mildoon showed himself at Merrihew. He had been passing, he said, and on an impulse had dropped by to see how things were going. Jaro conducted him into the drawing room. Mildoon, a middle-aged gentleman, somewhat sleek of torso and pallid of skin, was impeccably groomed and exuded a waft of expensive scent. He wore garments selected with an eye to conservative good taste

---

* Style: Indices too complicated to be enumerated here. The Style-rating enables astro-biologists to estimate at a glance the tolerance of the local environment to human habitancy.

leavened with intimations of cordiality, sincerity and unobtrusive high caste. A discreet emblem at his right hip indicated membership in the Zonkers: a sub-division of the Squared Circles. Over the years Mildoon had prospered exceedingly from shrewd and foresighted transactions in real property, but he professed himself never too preoccupied with large affairs to ignore smaller propositions such as Merrihew, and he so informed Jaro. He mentioned that he called once before on Luel Fath, but that Fath had decided not to sell, which — according to Mildoon — might have been a poor decision, since prices had recently taken something of a tumble and might drop lower yet.

"That is not good news," said Jaro.

Mildoon turned a rather disparaging glance around the room. The option of remodelling was always open to Jaro, but it was a risky business and Jaro might end up pouring money down a rathole — Mildoon had seen many such ventures come to grief — or he might simply reconcile himself to rattling around in a gloomy old barn. Or — here Mildoon performed an airy gesture — he might want to sell, and if so, Mildoon would bend the Association scale-book of values to its limit.

Jaro said that was nice of him, and how much did Mr. Mildoon have in mind.

Oh — possibly seventeen thousand, though Jaro must act quickly before the bottom fell out of the market.

"For the house and the property? The fifty acres of beautiful forest and meadow out there!"

Mildoon laughed incredulously. "Fifty acres of stone and muck is closer to truth! It's a breeding ground for snakes, stimps and leeches: sheer sorry wasteland."

It was a gloomy prospect, said Jaro. The price was not enough to cover the program he had in mind.

"How much then?" asked Mr. Mildoon idly.

"Oh — I don't know. We haven't arranged our figures yet. I was hoping for something closer to twenty-five or even thirty thousand."

Mildoon pretended to reel as if in shock. "With the best will in the world, we must be realistic; these are the stern facts of life. If I gave you as much as twenty, or even nineteen, my family would lock me away in a padded cell and rightly so!"

Jaro said that he was disappointed and that he would have to think things out.

Mildoon ruminated. "Let me see. I suppose I could noodle a bit here and doodle a bit there and take this rundown old place and the acreage off your hands; call it 'kindly benevolence', if you like. Essentially I'll be doing a favor for a young man in pathetic circumstances."

Mildoon smilingly shook his head. Jaro said: "Rundown or not, the house is where I can live, until I decide what to do with myself. In the meantime, the market may improve, or someone may make me a better offer."

"As you please," said Mildoon equably. He frowned toward the ceiling. "My time is worth money, and if you'll close the deal now, I'll go as high as twenty thousand. The price is good for about five minutes, then it drops again."

"I'm sorry, Mr. Mildoon, but I don't want to sell just now."

Mildoon departed with a composed face.

Halfway through the afternoon Jaro heard the quick thud of someone running up the front stairs and across the porch. Jaro cocked his head to listen. The rhythm of the sounds was not that of Skirl. When he opened the door, he found Lyssel smiling up at him. "Can I come in, Sir Orphan?"

Jaro looked her up and down. Lyssel, so it seemed, had decided to appear in her most provocative guise, which meant that she had some practical purpose in view. Still, Lyssel was Lyssel, who knew exactly how to enchant the minds of susceptible young men, and cause yearnings to rise all up and down their bodies. Today she wore dusky-white pantaloons, tight at the hips, loose at the ankles and a pink shirt; her hair was tied back in two impudent tufts tied with pink ribbons.

Jaro admitted her into the house, though with minimal cordiality, which she pretended not to notice.

Jaro said: "Lyssel, you surprise me. I haven't seen you for months. Now, out of nowhere you come frolicking into my life."

Lyssel put on a coquettish little grimace of wrinkled nose and pursed lips. "Jaro! Are you so insensitive? Memories are long in Thanet — though not permanent — for which you should be grateful."

Jaro's jaw dropped in bemusement. "Whatever for?"

Lyssel touched him lightly on the shoulder: a gesture signifying what? Forgiveness? Understanding? Affectionate complicity? As much or as little as Jaro wished to comprehend? She said gently: "It hasn't been all that long since you unleashed your gang of hired thugs upon poor Hanfer and his friends. That, you must know, set everyone's teeth on edge."

Jaro was thunderstruck. "My 'gang of thugs'? Where did you hear that?"

"From Hanfer, naturally. He said there were about six big ruffians armed with clubs."

"Ha! What a liar! Telephone him at this instant; explain that I will beat him senseless and break some more of his bones if he does not tell you the truth! I mean now and today!"

Lyssel shrugged, grinned, obeyed, and a furious Hanfer at last admitted that four 'Angels of Merciful Death' had attacked Jaro, and that he had thrashed them without any help.

"Well then!" said Lyssel, turning back to Jaro. "It's still no credit to you. I thought that you had handled them in a sensible and civilized fashion, without soiling your own hands, that would have been the way of a gentleman. Now it seems that you are as vicious a desperado as any."

"So it seems. Perhaps worse, now that I have learned the knack."

The corners of Lyssel's mouth jerked up. "I rather liked the dreamy Jaro who always seemed to be thinking far thoughts. Ah well, that was last year."

"And that is what you came to tell me?"

"Of course not! I heard the bad news and I thought I would see how you were coming along."

"The bad news has been bad for quite some time now. Your reactions are slow."

Lyssel gave an indignant toss of the head. "You have become the most sardonic person I know! If you weren't so handsome, it would be unbecoming, but I confess you only seem romantic, like a Mogadispian warrior prince."

"Well, yes," said Jaro. "That's how I feel when I talk to Hanfer. Otherwise, I feel as if I'm running just to stay in one place."

"And how are you doing, for a fact? Are you lonely?"

"I miss the Faths," said Jaro cautiously. "Otherwise, I'm not lonely."

"Hm," sighed Lyssel. "Poor Jaro! It must have been a terrible shock. But you were always something of a solitary person. Even just a little bit weird."

"Probably so."

Lyssel looked around the room, her expression not dissimilar to that of Norby Mildoon. She turned back to Jaro. "So: do you have definite plans?"

Jaro shrugged. "I won't be back at the Institute; that at least is definite."

"Jaro! What folly! You can't stop now! Soon you'll have your degree and a place in society: a Ring Nose or even — in time — a Squared Circle! It's not imposszible, you know!"

"I have other plans."

"So you may! But first comes the security of a prideful level in society!"

"You do not know me very well."

"I guess I don't. What other mistakes have I made?"

"You've made no mistakes. I am a mystery even to myself."

Lyssel came a step closer to him. "You are surrendering to a weakness. You can never rise in the world, until you focus upon reality!" She touched his shoulder.

"Ha!" laughed Jaro nervously. "What is reality?"

"You must sell this dreary old bat-trap for what you can get, and move into a smart little apartment near the Institute."

Jaro winced. "This place isn't so bad — and it's free."

"It lacks panache."

"So I have been told by Norby Mildoon, who doesn't seem to mind. He wants to buy with or without panache. Do you know him?"

"Of course! He's in Zonkers. He owns the *Pharsang* which is a beautiful space yacht which he never uses; in fact my Uncle Boven has offered him two hundred thousand sols for it, and Norby Mildoon will sell if his new scheme works out; in fact, that is undoubtedly why he wants to buy your property; you are right in the center of his development."

"He did not explain the details."

"It's to be a community of beautiful country estates for Circle types only. Your fifty acres separates him north from south, and he'll surely give you a decent price."

"The *Pharsang* must be quite a nice vessel."

"It is an absolutely splendid ship: a Falco Glitterway, and Norby has never really used it. I hope he sells to my Uncle Boven, because then we'll go on a cruise of the Pandora Chromatics, and the Polymarks and perhaps even down to Xanthenoros. Wouldn't that be wonderful?"

"Very wonderful. I'd like to come along. Do you think you could invite me?"

Lyssel grinned her impish grin. "I could invite you, but Boven Stamart would ask as to your Circle, and that would be the end of it."

"Even though he wants me to sell my property to Mildoon?"

"That's aside from the point. Don't forget, you'll surely get a generous price — probably more than the place is worth." Lyssel now placed her hands on both of his shoulders and looked up into his face with melting blue eyes. "You'll do as I ask, won't you?"

Prompted by curiosity, Jaro bent and kissed her. She responded willingly but without warmth. Jaro looked at her somberly, wondering what went on in her mind. She whispered: "You will sell to Norby and to no one else?"

Jaro said: "I'll sell wherever I get the best price."

Lyssel pouted. "But I want you to sell to Norby, so that Boven will buy the *Pharsang*. You'll do it, won't you, Jaro? For me?"

Jaro laughed. "You are part of the inducement?"

Lyssel raised her face. "Kiss me again, Jaro."

Jaro heard light footsteps approaching across the front porch. He jumped guiltily back from Lyssel, who watched him with a bemused smile, instantly aware of what was occurring. But she was clearly surprised to see Skirl Hutsenreiter enter the room. Skirl in her turn made no attempt to conceal her surprise upon finding Lyssel present.

Jaro found his voice. He spoke to Skirl. "I think that you may know Lyssel Bynnoc. She's a student at the Institute."

Skirl said: "I'm sure that I've seen her about. I'm afraid that I don't know her very well."

Jaro explained Lyssel's presence. "Lyssel's uncle — correct me,

Lyssel, if I get this wrong — wants to buy the *Pharsang* from Norby Mildoon, who desperately needs the money."

"Oh, not 'desperately'," said Lyssel. "He's very wealthy, and a Zonker."

"In any case, Mildoon is promoting a speculative enterprise and it so happens that Merrihew and my acreage is directly in the center of it. So, if I sell to Mildoon, he will have his property and then will sell the *Pharsang* to Lyssel's Uncle Boven who will take Lyssel on a wonderful cruise."

"How nice!" said Skirl.

"Yes, quite," said Lyssel. "So I came to make sure that Jaro would sell to no one but Mildoon."

Skirl looked at Jaro, mouth twisted in a cool half smile, head tilted back just a bit, eyes appraising. "And you were convinced by Lyssel's presentation?"

Jaro told Lyssel: "You may inform Norby Mildoon that I have changed my mind and that I will sell to him, if the price is right."

Lyssel showed him an uncertain smile. "You really will sell to Norby, then?"

"Certainly. Why not? I'm sure we can work out some sort of arrangement to suit us both."

Lyssel darted a glance toward Skirl, who now said stiffly: "Please excuse me; I must see to our supper." She left the room.

Lyssel looked after her in wonder. "She's living here — with you?"

"My status is apparently adequate," said Jaro.

Lyssel started toward the door. "I'll give Norby your message. He'll be happy to hear that you are being reasonable."

"Indeed. I am very reasonable."

As soon as Lyssel had gone, Jaro joined Skirl in the kitchen. Jaro thought that she seemed reserved. He told her of Norby Mildoon's call and of the information he had gained from Lyssel. "So it will all work out for the best, or so I hope."

"Hmf," said Skirl. "Lyssel is a vamp and a female scorpion. She'd do anything for a cruise to Xanthenoros."

Jaro gave his head a shake of pure innocence. "I'm sure I wouldn't know."

"I hope not," said Skirl severely.

After dinner Jaro reported the day's events to Tarr. He explained what he had in mind. Tarr endorsed his idea and agreed to cooperate in any way possible.

In the morning Jaro received a telephone call from Norby Mildoon, who addressed him with fulsome courtesy. "I understand that you might be willing to sell your property at a fair price?"

Jaro agreed that such was the case. "If you care to meet me here in about two hours, we can discuss the arrangements."

" 'Arrangements'?" asked Mildoon, with automatic suspicion. "What sort of arrangements? I hope you don't plan a lot of legalistic conditions of sale."

"Not at all. It should all be very simple."

"Good!" said Mildoon heartily. "I'll be there."

When Mildoon arrived, Jaro ushered him into the dining room, where Evan Tarr and Skirl sat at the table. Norby Mildoon halted, looked from one to the other.

Jaro performed introductions, which Mildoon acknowledged without enthusiasm. "Skirl Hutsenreiter is an effectuator; Evan Tarr is a technician. Please be seated."

Norby Mildoon wordlessly seated himself, as did Jaro. "Evan Tarr has prepared the papers which we will use for our negotiations."

Mildoon protested. "But I have the official forms here, ready for signature."

"Throw them away; our papers are better. They are simple, short, and comprehensive."

"Let me see them."

"There are two documents," said Jaro. "In a sense they are twins. One for you, one for me. You have a Glitterway space yacht, the *Pharsang*, for sale, so I understand?"

"That is true," snapped Norby Mildoon, impatient, yet reluctant to offend Jaro by a display of hauteur. "It was built by Falco Yards at Murchy and is the next thing to new. I just can't find time to enjoy it. But let us get on with our business."

Jaro smiled. "The Glitterway is our business. How much are you offering me for my house and acreage, which I am told is quite valuable?"

"Who told you that?" asked Mildoon sharply.

"No matter; what is your offer?"

Mildoon controlled his voice. "Twenty thousand sols, which is generous. The house needs complete renovation. The acreage is wild and rough."

"In that case I will pay you twenty thousand sols for the Glitterway. Here are the bills of sale. No money actually need change hands."

Mildoon looked at Jaro in stupefaction. "I have already turned down an offer of one hundred and eighty thousand sols."

"In that case, I will sell my house to you for two hundred thousand sols, and pay you the same amount for the Glitterway, and both of us will feel pleased with the bargain. You will be able to proceed with your development, and I will own the *Pharsang*, which I need."

Tarr said gravely: "Name whatever figures you prefer, Mr. Mildoon; we will enter the same amount upon each bill of sale, and the transaction will be completed in five minutes."

Mildoon jumped to his feet, face pink with rage. "This is a barefaced swindle! You can't do this to me!"

Skirl said: "You have already spent over half a million sols on your development."

"And where, may I ask, did you hear this figure?"

"Certain elements of the financial community would like to be Clam Muffins. I control a black ball."

Norby Mildoon, who had made as if to pound the table, stopped short, fist in mid-air. He stared at Skirl. "If you are a Clam Muffin, what are you doing in a place like this?"

"I could ask the same question of you," said Skirl.

"Let us return to business," said Jaro. "You have heard my price; it is firm. If you do not take it, I will convert Merrihew into a rustic tavern which should do very well."

Mildoon wrangled another five minutes, then gracelessly acceded to Jaro's terms. "I have no choice; I can recognize a cul-de-sac when I see one. Bring out your papers; I will sign. The Glitterway is yours."

After Mildoon had signed, and the transaction was complete, he said in a voice of hollow triumph: "I lost my spaceyacht, but in the end I will gain back twenty times its value! You could have held me up for double what you got."

"No matter," said Jaro. "We are not avaricious."

Jaro, Evan Tarr and Skirl went aboard the magnificent Falco Glitterway. Tarr, ordinarily matter-of-fact and even impassive, was hard-put to restrain his enthusiasm. "This is large enough to move passengers or freight. In short, you have a source of income about like that of a full professor."

"Perhaps a bit more precarious," said Skirl.

"I don't know whether the Faths would approve the use to which I have put Merrihew," mused Jaro. "I rather suspect not. In any case, I owe them all my gratitude."

There was further conversation. Jaro mentioned that he would probably need a crew, to assist in the operation of the vessel. "I hope to enlist two or three persons with very special qualifications: a First Officer, a Chief Engineer and perhaps a steward. The First Officer should be a person of superlative intelligence, clever, versatile, quick-thinking, a person of high status — even a Clam Muffin, if we could find one. As for the Chief Engineer he must be a man of long experience, crafty, resourceful and something of a vagabond. A steward may or may not be necessary."

Skirl asked thoughtfully: "When are you taking applications?"

"At any time."

"You made no mention of salary."

"Salaries will be sparse at first, until I find out what happened on Kammerwelt. When and if the *Pharsang* turns a profit, salaries will improve. My income will feed us and buy cheap wine, but I can't overextend myself, since I already have an effectuator on the payroll."

"The effectuator is working for nothing," said Skirl. "It seems as if your crew will be doing the same. Nevertheless, I apply for the position of First Officer."

Tarr said: "I apply for the position of Chief Engineer. Salary is of no great consequence. After we straighten out your affairs, then we'll go into the space-transport business, if you're still so inclined. I have had considerable experience along these lines; in fact I was once captain of my own ship, but that is long ago, and much has happened since then. As far as the *Pharsang* is concerned, it's your ship. You shall be captain, Skirl the First Officer, and I will sign on as engineer, cook, roustabout, navigator, general dog's-body, and strategist. We will share profits, if any occur. Does this arrangement suit you?"

"I couldn't be more pleased."

Chapter 5

1.

Close to the remote edge of the Gaean Reach, in the sector known as 'the Dragon's Maw', Robert Palmer's Star shone brilliant and white, its corona flaring with films of blue, red and green color. A dozen planets danced attendance, like children careening around a maypole, but only the world Kammerwelt knew that narrow range of conditions tolerant to human existence.

Though remote, the Dragon's Maw had been explored during early times, by rogue locators, pirates and fugitives; Kammerwelt had been settled for many thousands of years. Four continents, islands, oceans and seas defined the topography; the flora and fauna, as always, had evolved into forms of unique particularity, the fauna having attained such a bizarre variety, with habits so startling and destructive that two continents had been designated as preserves, where the creatures, large and small, biped or otherwise, could hop, pounce, lumber, run, rumble, pillage and grind others to bits or tear them apart, as met their needs. On the other two continents the fauna had been suppressed.

The human population of Kammerwelt had been derived from many sources which, rather than merging, had clotted into a number of stubbornly discrete units, based upon cultural factors, occupation, race and simple wrong-headedness. Across thousands of years the differentiation had proceeded to a point where Kammerwelt had become an inexhaustible fount of information for anthropologists of all types; so the Faths had come to record the music of the Wildenberry Steppes. The archives at Thanet Institute gave no detailed information as to their itinerary, save to mention the Wildenberry Steppe and the village Stronk.

The largest city of Kammerwelt was Tanzig. Like several other cities of Kammerwelt, Tanzig had been built to the dictates of a precise plan. Concentric rings of buildings surrounded a central plaza, where three bronze statues a hundred feet tall stood facing away from each other, arms raised in gestures whose purport had long been forgotten.*

Jaro, Skirl and Tarr landed the *Pharsang* at the Tanzig spaceport. The voyage from Thanet had been pleasant, or, thought Jaro, not overtly unpleasant, since the commodious *Pharsang* allowed each of the travellers as much privacy as he or she desired. It gradually became clear to Jaro that Skirl was not easy with Evan Tarr. He could not understand the nature or the cause of her feeling with any certainty. Dislike? Distrust? Suspicion? Doubt? None of these seemed to fit. Jaro remembered that Skirl was a life-long Clam Muffin and that Evan Tarr was a vagabond; was this the basis for her coolness? Possibly; who could say? Perhaps not even Skirl herself. If Tarr sensed the coolness — as he probably did, thought Jaro — he kept his own counsel and treated Skirl with the same casual low-key courtesy that he used toward Jaro.

The three passed through the Tanzig space terminal and entered the disheveled old town with its cocked roofs and twisted clapboard siding. Nothing Jaro saw or heard struck any note of familiarity.

Returning to the *Pharsang*, they unshipped the flitter and flew a thousand miles east to the village Stronk, at the edge of the Wildenberry Steppe, then north along a road bordering the steppe on the right hand, and the dun Wyching Hills to the left.

Jaro had now become attentive; chills moved along the skin of his back. Here was significant ground, steeped with baleful memories; he could almost feel the heat of the sunlight on his bare skin, the abrasions on his knees, then the hoarse shouts and fear, which clamped at his guts. Then there in the road the taste of dust in his mouth, while around him danced thick peasant legs, and sticks beat thud! thud! thud! on his back. For an instant the recollection was vivid; he pointed to a spot on the road. "There."

---

* Early chronicles declared that the three statues represented the same individual: the fabled justiciary and lawgiver David Alexander, depicted in three typical poses: summons to judgment, quelling of the rabble, and imposition of equity.

Tarr landed the flitter; the three alighted and looked around the landscape. The sunlight beat upon their heads. To the west the hills showed the color of dead jointgrass.

Jaro walked a few paces along the road, then halted. "I think it was about here that the Faths found me."

"And where did you come from?"

"I think from over the hills. A river, a thicket of reeds. I can almost smell them. If I listen, I hear the echo of my mother's voice." Jaro thought back across the years. "There was a man standing against the twilight. I became frightened. My mother was frightened. There was confusion; something happened; she told me something. I can almost remember." Jaro squinted toward the hills. "She put me into a boat, and the next thing I knew I was swimming through the dark. After that — nothing."

Skirl touched Jaro's arm. "Look."

A few hundred feet down the road stood a trio of squat young peasants, eyes small and black in moony faces. They gave no signal of greeting, and stared with impersonal curiosity. Skirl said softly: "These might have been the persons who beat you."

"They are about the right age," said Jaro tonelessly.

"Aren't you angry with them?"

"Very angry. But I don't think I'll do anything about it."

Evan Tarr strolled down the road and spoke to the men. They responded with a curious form of exaggerated deference, more mocking than real. Tarr returned. "They say they don't remember the episode. But they are lying — not out of fear, but for the sheer enjoyment of misleading an off-worlder. It's common enough."

"There's nothing to be learned here," said Jaro.

The three rode the flitter aloft, and the landscape of Kammerwelt spread below — to the east the great plain, an expanse, of ocher, daubed with streaks of dull red; in the far distance, pencilings of black and brown. To the south ferngrass trees concealed the village Stronk. To the north a dozen farms occupied the fringe of the steppe. At the far side of the Wyching Hills a river flowed looping and curving from the west to veer at the hills and disappear into the northern haze. At a distance of five miles a small town occupied a site near the river.

According to the flitter map, the town was Point Extase: a name which meant nothing to Jaro.

Jaro, Skirl and Evan Tarr flew west, following the river to Point Extase. They circled above the town, which was only slightly larger than Stronk, though more oppressed by the erosion of years. Most of the structures were built of horizontal strips of clapboard, painted in any one of a hundred soft colors. The material, split from the stems of grass which grew two hundred feet high in the jungles, was light, durable, cheap, and ubiquitous, though it tended to warp with age, so that the structures of Point Extase had a rumpled look, with their roofs askew, like the hats of drunken old harridans. In total perspective, Point Extase was not without a certain quaint charm.

The town was separated from the river by a strip of swampy waste-land half a mile wide, overgrown in part by thickets of tall reedy grass. On a patch of open ground between the reeds and the river Jaro noticed an old yellow house, which instantly aroused a warm shock of recognition. He pointed. "That is the place. I am sure of it!"

The flitter landed; the three alighted and approached the old house. The roof sagged to right and left in a woebegone manner; the house itself was boarded up and in a state of dilapidation. The clapboard walls had at one time been painted yellow; the paint was now peeling and flaking. The house had long been abandoned; the doors were locked, but Jaro had no wish to enter. Emotions caused his skin to prickle, as he stood staring at the front elevation of the house, at once strange and familiar. Into his mind came a spurt of insight. Of course! he told himself, it was my destiny to come here! I have been brought here willy-nilly; I was impelled; no matter what my state of ignorance or reluctance or stagnation: still I would have been forced to come! I convinced myself that if I came to Kammerwelt I could finally extinguish the voice in my mind, but this is unreasonable; it was a sop to my logic. I came because of a compulsion; if it wasn't one reason it would have been another. Why? Perhaps I am about to know. As he looked toward the house present time became remote and he seemed to be looking down a tunnel of time. He saw the house; the paint was a fresher yellow and the door was open. He heard a voice, and he knew it to be the voice of his mother. She stood before him; he could feel her nearness but he could not see her face. She was speaking to him, and he heard the words clearly: "Jaro! Be brave and faithful! I weave these words into the stuff of your brain; they will unravel when you stand on this spot, as you must, for I will place the command upon you. As of now, hide this box in your den, where no one will know. Then, when you are strong and capable, you must return here and take back this box. You will then learn the charge I put upon you. It is harsh and it is terrible; still it must be."

In response Jaro heard what he knew to be his own voice, coming as if from a great distance: "I will do my best."

Jaro became aware of Skirl's presence close beside him, her face anxious. "Jaro! What is happening to you? Jaro? Are you well? Can you hear me?"

Jaro drew a deep breath. He discovered that tears were coming from his eyes. "I can hear you, at least." Skirl started to speak again, then fell silent as Jaro, moving like a somnambulist, walked slowly around the house, pausing every three or four steps. He seemed to come to a decision and went to a small half-ruined stone shed. His face blank, his eyes unfocussed, he dropped to his hands and knees, crept into the shed, where he groped at the base of the wall. He backed out of the shed, stood erect, and now he was holding a black metal document box.

Tarr and Skirl approached him and waited as Jaro emerged from his abstracted state. At last he looked from one to the other. "I heard my mother's voice — as if she were speaking to me in a dream. She told me to get this box."

"I think that your mother put a hypnotic command into your mind," said Evan Tarr.

Jaro nodded. "It must be so, and much is explained. But not everything."

"Let's look into the box."

The three went to sit on the sagging porch. Jaro opened the box. It contained an envelope folded from weatherproof parchment, attached to an accompanying letter. For the second time, Jaro read a letter addressed to him by someone who had loved him and now was dead. The letter had clearly been scribbled in haste and in the extremity of emotion.

"Who am I addressing? I hope that it is Jaro who reads this letter. But I cannot see down the long years and who knows whose curious eyes will read these words, or how far in the future. Jaro, I will try to place a pattern on your mind, to bring you back to this place, and if you live, it may succeed, or it may not. When you learn the facts, you will know that I could have done nothing else; so if you resent the coercion, forgive me please!

"Now I am desperate. I have waited too long; I have seen Asrubal. He will soon find us, and then life will be gone. Our eyes will be numb; we will see not even blackness; we will hear not even silence; we will fear not even the unimaginable! Jaro, what a queer fact, and it makes me shiver to think of it. If I survive, you will never read this letter. Since you are reading it you will know that events went badly, at least for me. But I expect nothing else, and I grieve only that I must place this burden on you. It is too late to justify or explain, except I will say this: Asrubal is the feared one! He will have killed me, and he has killed your father, since three years have gone by, and what of poor Garlet?

These are your instructions; follow them if you are able.

The envelope contains a document which will destroy Asrubal. Make several copies of this document. Store a copy at the Commercial Bank of Tanzig. Tender the original to the Natural Bank at Mibbs, on Gadron. At least one of the copies must be transmitted by the best means available to Romarth on Maz and there displayed to the high authorities; another delivered to the Master of Hoy House.

"To this end, go to Mibbs on Gadron. Be vigilant! Do not deal with Lorquin Shipment; you will be killed and thrown into space, since Lorquin is an agency of Hoy House: which is to say, Asrubal.

Consult Yamb at the Primrose Consolidators. Safeguard the remaining copies of the document at your best discretion.

If Primrose is no longer shipping to Maz, be stealthy and devious; the danger is great since you can trust no one.

Maz is a very old world; it is wild and dangerous, where your father met his death. At Romarth, Hoy House is evil, as is Asrubal. Ask Yamb about conditions on Maz. Remember, Asrubal will kill you with pleasure. It has been three years since your father went to

Maz on an impossible mission; it is probably Asrubal who has killed him. Beware the Loclor riders; they are cruel and have no concept of human sentiment. Enter no ruined cities of the forest, nor old manses, by reason of house ghouls who now infest such places. Last, and of the greatest importance. Learn what you can of Garlet. Discover his fate; help him if possible; avenge him if necessary.

As I look at you I am heartsick, for now we will part. I love this brave little morsel of life named Jaro; I look across the room and see you as you are now, so earnest and handsome; you are wondering why I write so sadly, and when you read this letter you will know. My poor little Jaro, and worse: the poor miserable Garlet, who has been the one to suffer, who must be yours to help, though by the time you read this, all hope will be gone. I have finished the letter. Now I will put a force on your mind, to bring you back to this desperate place. You may not know why you are coming or what brings you here, but come you must.

I can write no more. My love goes with you always. Even if I am gone, it will persist, and perhaps you will feel it. If you listen, it might even give you counsel. I have often wondered about such things. I wish I could give you news of your father — but I have none; he is lost and gone, somewhere on Maz. If anyone knows, it will be Asrubal. If you go to seek him, first you must go to Mibbs on Gadron. When Asrubal learns of your coming, as eventually he must, you will be protected only by the documents you now hold. He will know that you have the means to destroy him, and he will try to deal with you first! So take care! I can say no more.

Your mother, Jamile.

For a time no one spoke. Then Skirl said: "Poor brave woman! So she was killed!"

Jaro found that tears were welling down his cheeks, and that the sunlight seemed to have gone gray and desolate. Evan Tarr said gruffly: "It is a melancholy letter."

Jaro opened the heavy brown envelope and withdrew the contents. There were a dozen pages of what appeared to be commercial accounts and a bank draft. He gave the papers a cursory inspection, returned them to their envelope and the three returned to Tanzig's central plaza. At the District Agency of Vital Statistics, they discovered that fifteen years before a woman known as Jan May, resident at the address of the yellow clapboard house at the back of Point Extase, had been found dead in the river, the victim of unspecified foul play. Her son, age five years, was missing and presumed drowned.

They returned to the street. Jaro said bleakly: "She saved me; then she was set upon and killed. Asrubal did the killing. I wonder why."

"If he were trying to take these papers, he failed," said Skirl. "But they would appear to be his motive."

The three went to a cafe at the side of the square, in the slanting afternoon sunlight; here they examined the documents which Jamile had entrusted to Jaro's care. Tarr said: "The draft seems viable, so far as I can determine. It is drawn upon the account of Hoy House at the Natural Bank and payable on demand to the bearer, along with any incremental interest. The total should be something more than three hundred thousand sols: certainly enough to embarrass Asrubal."

Skirl asked: "And these other papers? They seem to be invoices or bills of lading, or something similar."

Jaro studied them. "They mean nothing to me."

"Still, Jamile wanted them taken to Romarth, wherever that is," said Skirl.

"So she did," said Jaro. "I would like to oblige her, though I am fifteen years late."

"Fifteen years ago there's not much you could have done."

"True. Now conditions are different, and I will keep faith with my poor mother, if I possibly can."

"That is a reasonable program," said Tarr. "It is also dangerous."

Jaro nodded. "So I expect. I do not intend to involve either you or Skirl, so we must part company for a time."

Skirl said tartly, "When I become frightened I will let you know. Meanwhile, I am an effectuator and must take the good with the bad."

Evan Tarr leaned back in his chair and looked off across the square. He said in a flat voice: "The time has come when I must speak with candour; it is not easy. For me secrecy is more natural than breathing. But now the time has come." He paused to order his thoughts. "It comes to this: I have an agenda of my own which I have not troubled to describe, since it runs more or less parallel with your own. There are at least four reasons why I intend to participate in this affair. First, when we are finished, I would hope to engage the *Pharsang* in commercial transport, serving remote ports-of-call. It is a pleasant life, never monotonous and often profitable; I know this from experience. If for no other reason, I am anxious to keep you alive. Second: I find Asrubal's conduct offensive; I consider him an enemy and I want to see him dead. Thirdly, we are friends, and it is now that you need my help. Fourthly — but this I will keep to myself; three reasons should be enough."

Jaro spoke stiffly. "Naturally, I am grateful to you both for your support."

"Then we need say no more."

"Except that you have made me curious. What was the fourth reason?"

"For now it need not concern us, perhaps it never will, and if not, so much the better."

2.

The world Gadron orbited a yellow dwarf of advanced age, whose name had been forgotten, and which perhaps had never even been catalogued in *Stellar Objects Of the Gaean Reach*. However, according to the more or less authoritative *Handbook of the Planets*, Gadron's sun had originally been named Yellow Rose by the legendary Wilbur Wailey*.

---

* Wilbur Wailey, after a stint as locator, began to conduct enterprises of a questionable sort. His supreme achievement was that of 'empire-builder'; he located a world so far Beyond and so lost among the clusters and wisps and stellar arms that, ten thousand years later, it still had not been rediscovered.

To this world, which Wailey named Sybilla, he introduced a population of handsome young women, whom he recruited by a variety of means. Some he paid generous bonuses; others he kidnapped, from convents, colleges, holiday camps, beauty pageants, spiritual improvement groups, and the like. On one occasion he captured an all-girl fife, bugle and drum corps, along with their instruments. A few months later he induced six hundred and fifteen Prime Type A Virgins of the Pellucid Eleusis to board his ship. They disembarked, like all the others, upon the world Sybilla where one by one, carefully,

Gadron, illuminated by the light of Yellow Rose, wandered across an empty gulf near the edge of the galaxy, in a region almost forgotten by the rest of the Reach. The population of Gadron tended to cluster in four zones, each centered upon a small town, all in the northern hemisphere and well away from the belt of equatorial desert which girdled the planet. This strip of desert was segmented like the links of a sausage, with channels connecting a pair of shallow oceans to north and south. The deserts flowed with odd oily rivers originating in forests with purple and black stalks, supporting persimmon-colored parasol-pads. On the pads large lizard-like beings danced and gyrated, leapt from pad to pad, and sometimes built tall conical structures of fiber and mucilage thirty feet high. Through small round windows the lizards thrust their heads, looked to right and left, then jerked back into the darkness.

Exactly along the equator a curtain of perpetual rain hung from a high wall of black clouds, constantly fed by tradewinds from south and north, sweeping together, colliding, rising high to the upper atmosphere, to curl over and flow back the way it had come. The swamps along the fringes of the desert and beside the rivers seethed with life. Balls of tangled white worms; prancing web-footed andromorphs with green gills and eyes at the end of long stalks; starfish-like pentapods tiptoeing on limbs twenty feet long; creatures all maw and tail; wallowing hulks of cartilage with pink ribbed undersides: such were the creatures who inhabited the swamps of Gadron.

On the continent Caro were the four inhabited districts. At Mibbs, largest of the towns, was the spaceport, the commercial nodes, and

---

methodically, assiduously Wilbur Wailey got each of them with child — not once, but several times. Fifteen years later he made the rounds again, this time inseminating his daughters with neither prejudice nor favoritism; as he did his grand-daughters in the sunset of his life.

When anthropologists gather for a gossip or an excursion into shop talk in the lounges of their clubs, sometimes late in the evening after several tots of Pusser's Regulation or Old Tanglefoot have been consumed, someone may well make a reference to Wilbur Wailey and his energetic career. After a few moments someone will say: "They don't make men like Wilbur Wailey nowadays!" And for a time the conversation will quiet, while everyone thinks his or her own thoughts and wonders how it goes now on far Sybilla.

a population of eight thousand individuals, most of whom lived by a low-key philosophy, which renounced haste, tension, and strident ambition. Visitors often spoke enviously of the 'unflappable sang-froid' which they had discovered at Mibbs. Others, of a different temperament used such terms as 'apathy' to describe the same conduct.

The structures of Mibbs, when viewed as a group, created an effect which was unique, though no individual structure by itself seemed remarkable. The architecture was uniform: walls of concreted fiber and glass, capped by flat low domes, surmounted by iron devices combining the functions of weather vane, aesthetic motif and ghost chaser. Commercial enterprises lined the main street: the Natural Bank, the Fragrant Party Hotel, Cudder's Market, Lorquin Shipping Agents, Tecmart, the Peurifoy Refreshment Parlor, and further along the street, the Primrose Consolidators. Dendrons grew in the back yards and open spaces, casting shade and exhaling a dry peppery odor.

The *Pharsang* landed at the Mibbs spaceport. Jaro, Skirl and Tarr alighted, complied with a few formalities at the terminal office and were given the freedom of the town. They found themselves at the head of a broad avenue which traversed the full extent of Mibbs, and eventually disappeared into a forest of gaunt puff-wad dendrons, mustard-ocher of stalk and black of pad, the colors muted both by distance and the lazy saffron light of Yellow Rose Star.

The three paused to survey the street. They took note of the eccentric, rather cramped, architecture and the general air of lassitude — which might or might not be deceptive. Certainly, thought Jaro, there seemed something hushed and unreal in the atmosphere which gave the town Mibbs its character. Fifteen years ago his father had walked this street, then had vanished. According to Jamile, he was dead. Jaro wondered how and where.

Local time was about noon, to judge by the altitude of Yellow Rose. It shone without dazzle, producing a serene light which played odd tricks with perspective. The streets of Mibbs were quiet. The town folk moved sedately about their affairs, slippers gliding silently across the pavement. Some walked with heads bent, arms clasped behind their backs, as if engrossed in abstract calculation. Others paused to rest on benches where they contemplated their plans for the day. They showed themselves as neither gregarious nor voluble. When two persons passed on the street, they gave each other suspicious side-glances under hooded eyelids. When friends or business associates met and communication was necessary, first they looked right and left, over their shoulders, then spoke in guarded undertones, as if they imparted matter of secret import. On this basis, Mibbs seemed a veritable hive of intrigue. Probably, thought Jaro, this was not truly the case.

As the three watched, a flight of long-billed birds, pink with black crests rising along their necks, passed overhead. Their wings, narrow and of remarkable span from tip to tip, were flapped almost negligently. As they flew, they issued a succession of discordant calls — the loudest sounds to be heard across Mibbs.

As Jaro looked along the main street of Mibbs, he remembered Jamile's warnings. They were in a dangerous environment, she had implied, but if danger existed, it was not immediately in evidence. Mibbs seemed the definition of tranquility, though the atmosphere of stealth and convert communication created a tension — if one were sensitive to such influences.

Standing across the street from the Lorquin Shipping Agency, they looked through glass panels into an apparently conventional office. At a counter to the back stood a small thin-faced man with a fringe of white hair ringing a bald pink pate. Could this be the dreaded Asrubal? Jaro thought not.

A hundred yards further along the avenue the Primrose Consolidators occupied a small office, with a single glass pane. Jaro asked Tarr: "What is a 'consolidator'? I've been wondering since I first heard the word."

"A 'consolidator' does whatever someone pays him to do," was Tarr's response. "He is like an effectuator who limits himself to financial transactions: brokerage, import, export, transshipment, smuggling: anything profitable. The consolidator tries to create reasons for others to give him money, and is often amazingly inventive. I tried my hand at it once but could not bring the pieces together, and went back to hauling cargo."

In the Primrose office, the clerk sat at a desk: a tall somber woman, parchment-pale, with a mop of black hair cut short at ear level with a brutal lack of finesse. Her face was triangular and dominated by a harsh nose and a dreary mouth.

It was decided that Jaro should enter the office and ask where to find Aubert Yamb.

Jaro hesitated. "What reason do I give when she asks what I want to see him about?"

"Tell her politely that Mr. Yamb might not want you to discuss his private affairs with the world at large."

Jaro entered the office. A placard on the desk read

Dame Ebezitra Pidy
Executive Manager

Dame Pidy gave Jaro a cool stare. "Yes, sir?"

"I have some business with Mr. Aubert Yamb. Where can I find him?"

Dame Pidy spoke indifferently. "He is in poor health; so you will discover for yourself. His house is 'Antel's Song', the second to the left down Titwillow Lane."

The three found the house: a cottage deep in the shade of six aromatic black dendrons with heart-shaped blue and acid-green pads. Four interlocking concrete cubes at ground level supported two others, which were capped by a flat dome, after the quaint local style: such was Aubert Yamb's residence.

At the front entrance they were met by a slatternly obese woman with lank hair and a scowling pudgy face. She wore the usual oddments of multi-colored panels and shawls which seemed to be the current vogue at Mibbs, with feet encased in slippers of riveted and jointed bands of black iron. She spoke sharply: "You have come to the wrong place; our quota is under dispute, and in any case it has long been oversubscribed."

"That is good to hear," said Tarr. "Where is Aubert Yamb?"

"You shall not take him away again; he is ailing and seriously unfit."

"A pity. Explain to him that old friends have come to see him and ask after his financial situation."

"I can tell you myself!" the woman grumbled. "It is in poor condition. Go through the door; his eyes are dim; he cannot see and he suffers a pithismuratic ague."

The three visitors found Yamb lying flat on his back, staring toward the ceiling. The room was dark and heavy with the odors of disease and soiled cloth.

Jaro introduced himself and said he wanted to learn of events long past — fifteen or even twenty years ago. Yamb spoke freely, in a dreary monotone. "Twenty years ago — that is when my troubles began! At that time I worked as Director at Lorquin Agency, behind the counter where old Pounter stands today. I earned a wage but never enough; like all men I was avaricious. My opportunity floated down from the sky."

Yamb's opportunity was the *Distilcord*, a tramp space freighter of moderate size which had arrived with a mixed cargo of small tools, pharmaceuticals and informational materials. The cargo, by reason of several defalcations, attempted swindles, two assassinations and other circumstances, had become the property of the *Distilcord*, Captain Maihac, and his chief mate Evan Tarr.

Yamb had recently been discharged from his post at Lorquin Shipping by Asrubal, for offenses he declared to be trivial if not imaginary. He immediately secured a comparable post with Primrose Consolidators. While working at Lorquin, he had often loaded the agency's space freighter *Dubar* with similar goods, and he mentioned to Maihac that there always seemed to be a ready market for such stuffs, at a good price, at Romarth on Maz.

Maihac showed interest in the idea, and asked for more information. Where was Romarth? Nearby? He had never heard of such a place.

"For a good reason!" Yamb told him. "Romarth is nearby to nowhere. It is a city alone, and is as old as time."

"That is interesting, but not too definite."

"Most of what I know is indefinite. Romarth has always been a mystery: now, in the past and probably forever!"

Maihac laughed incredulously. "So where is this city of mystery?"

"On Maz there is a dark forest. It covers half of a continent. The forest surrounds Romarth."

"So where is Maz?"

Yamb gestured toward the sky. "It lies out yonder in the void. The original locator is not known; the records have been forgotten and lost. Perhaps it was the legendary locator Polydor Shimmel, who was at the very least an original thinker, and quite possibly mad. Most locators would go to the edge of the Reach and very timidly make a small sweep into the near-Beyond, then scurry back into the Reach before they were noticed. Not Shimmel, if it truly were he. The edge of anything was to Shimmel only the beginning, and the end of each beginning was a new beginning. He travelled far and still farther, as if he would travel forever — out past the Reach, past the Beyond, then beyond the Beyond and out into the void where he found nothing but the glimmer of one last star. He named this star Nightlamp, and its lonely world, Maz, for reasons unknown, though it is said that Maz was the ancient Silurian devil who guarded the door to the afterworld. But this all happened so very long ago, at the beginnings of Gaean civilization; there was no settlement of Gadron until much later. But Romarth persists. The Lorquin freighter *Dubar* carries goods to the port of entry, and Asrubal fearlessly enriches himself, since all are too proud to take heed of money. They have naught in their minds but pride and honour."

The obese woman interrupted the tale: "And so they should pay for the privilege! Here at Mibbs we know how to deal with folk that puts on airs, or runs about helter-skelter trying to gain a march on ordinary folk! If the high-leg plutarchs of Romarth are too proud to ask the cost, then let them pay!"

Skirl asked: "And how do they pay? What goods do they export?"

"They export not a whit!" said Yamb. "They have investments across the Reach: great old fortunes which have floated them on tides of wealth for ten thousand years. They live like the kings of kings! I was meant for such a life, but see me now: at the edge of destitution."

Skirl demanded: "How do you know so much about Asrubal?"

Yamb showed a knowing grin. "When I managed Lorquin, I dealt with his invoices and bills of lading. There I learned that the factor Asrubal buys on the cheap and sells at the dear."

On sudden thought Jaro brought out copies of Jamile's documents. He held them before Yamb's eyes. "Can you read these?"

"Aye, just barely; my sight is not what it was once."

"Do you recognize these papers?"

"Indeed I do. They are invoices the factor Asrubal submitted to the

Disbursary at Romarth. Attached is a notation as to Asrubal's costs, which are, of course, disproportionate. But at Romarth there is money enough, and it is considered beneath Roum dignity to inquire as to costs. One measures only honour at Romarth."

"So much for that," said Skirl. "One mystery is solved."

Jaro asked: "Did you ever meet a woman named Jamile?"

"Yes, a tragic tale!"

The fat woman said: "You are tiring poor Yamb and taking up my valuable time. Do you intend compensation?"

"Nonsense," said Tarr. "We are doing you a favor by visiting you and talking about old times. If anything, you should be preparing a feast to mark the occasion."

Yamb laughed. "At least you have brought me a moment of amusement. What do you wish to know? About Jamile? It started with Maihac, as I mentioned. We thought we could out-flank Asrubal and sell direct to Romarth, but he turned ugly. To make a long story short, I was beaten and threatened, while Maihac was killed and who knows what happened to the *Distilcord*?"

"And Jamile?"

Yamb groaned and complained that his throat was dry. "Have we no sifus to drink?" he demanded peevishly of the fat woman. "Is life to be lived and sifus drank deep only after we are dead? Bring out the bottle, woman! Pour with a willing hand! This is a great day; I remember none like it — fancy that: not even so miserable a celebration as this! — for years."

The woman, tight-lipped, poured out tots of a yellow-green liquor, which tasted of aromatic pollen and left a tingle on the tongue.

Yamb smacked his lips. "That is the real stuff! Now, as to Jamile, I know almost nothing. Maihac and his mate took the *Distilcord* to Maz and there he was killed. Two years later, more or less, the mate — his name was Maihac, so I recall —"

Skirl asked: "Dain Maihac?" She darted a quick look toward Evan Tarr, and Jaro thought with a pang, that any negative feeling Skirl felt toward Tarr must now be reinforced.

" 'Dain' Maihac," muttered Yamb. "Aye, so it was. He returned aboard the *Distilcord* with Jamile and her child, a boy two years old. He put them aboard a passenger packet, and went back to Maz, and I saw him no more."

Aubert Yamb paused in his dreary recitation. "There is much I don't know; but it would seem that events went in a certain direction, as evidenced by the aftermath."

Jaro and Tarr waited while Yamb collected his thoughts. "It is all very strange — but what could be more strange than the way of life on Romarth?" He pointed a trembling finger toward the ceiling. "Even now, out yonder, by the light of Nightlamp, events still continue by these reckonings. The Loclor dance across the Prycene Steppes, and the house-ghouls wander through the old palaces, venturing out to take up children."

"So — what more do you know?"

Yamb made a gesture as if to move aside all the irrelevant clutter of the past. "It is long ago, and my mind has started to wander. I look up into the darkness and I seem to see moving shapes, delineating old events, but as often as not they are random thoughts, which I must ignore. In truth, I cannot altogether trust my memory."

"You seem to be doing very well," said Tarr. "What else can you tell us?"

"I have illusions! My wife Ilya comes in and speaks, and I hear her voice as if she were the beautiful maiden, so shy and trusting, that once I knew! Then I blink and the apparatus of time works its mischief to destroy what I suppose are actually the pitiful pleadings of my brain. When I peer about with my last glimmers of sight, I find only a few ponderous and implacable symbols — I shall call what I see symbols —"

Here Yamb's brooding wife Ilya interposed a contemptuous admonition: "Come, come, Yamb; these folk are not all agog to hear your dithyrambs. Speak to the point, like a man!"

"No doubt, my dear, no doubt," said Yamb. "Still, let us admit that in the best of all possible worlds, I would be served both ramp and pot-cheese with my gruel and show a fine leg as I danced."

"You are a complete visionary," muttered Ilya. "Why are you not happy with what you have? There are many dead people who would gladly change places with you."

"It gives one to wonder," mused Yamb.

Ilya grumbled: "Put the idea out of your mind; it's hard enough taking care of you, as you are."

Jaro asked: "Illusions apart, what more can you tell us?"

Yamb heaved a fretful sigh. "It was long ago; Dain Maihac brought Jamile and his son to Mibbs and sent them somewhere offworld, where they would be safe. Maihac returned to Maz; he was now alone in the *Distilcord*, since his mate Evan Tarr had been killed."

"Why did he do this?"

"To do a deed of gallant rescue! When the cavaliers of Hoy invaded the Sadaj palace they had tried to seize Jamile as a hostage; when they failed they took a certain Garlet instead, and clapped him into prison. There he would stay, forever until Asrubal was vindicated with all estaing restored. Jamile wanted me to go with Maihac, but I could not; I feared capture by the Loclor; they would take me hopping stiff-leg to their garmatic music, off and away across the steppe, and while I danced and careened and jigged and whirled, just so long would they allow me my life. Such are the Loclor; I wanted none of them, and Maihac went off alone in the *Distilcord*. Jamile took passage in a Voynitz Line packet, but where she went I cannot say, nor do I know her fate, nor that of her son.

"Only this remains to be told: some time later — three or four years — I saw Asrubal in the Lorquin office, he was neither dead nor lacking in estaing, and I knew that Dain Maihac had failed, and was dead. Asrubal went off-world in a Voynitz packet. I suspected that he had gone to look for Jamile, that he might kill her and her child. That is how things go at this far place."

3.

Jaro, Skirl and Evan Tarr sat at a table on the terrace in front of the Hotel Peurifoy, in the shade of gaunt maroon and mustard-ocher dendrons. "The time has come," said Tarr, "when I must tell you what I know. You will wonder why I waited, why I concealed my identity until now. There are a dozen reasons, some simple, some complicated. I won't try to explain any of them. I did what I thought easiest and best, and I am still of that opinion."

Jaro studied him with a fresh appraisal. "Evan Tarr the vagabond! You are my father!"

"Perhaps you hoped for someone respectable?"

"No," said Jaro. "Everything considered, I am content."

Skirl gave a sardonic snort. "Naturally. You are two of a kind. But —"

"Yes, I know," said Dain Maihac. "I have many explanations to make."

Chapter 6

1.

While still a young man, Dain Maihac had come into possession of the *Distilcord*, a space freighter of something under moderate size, old but still strong and serviceable. With his chief mate, comrade and de facto partner, he kept to an irregular schedule, carrying cargoes of opportunity among the seldom-visited ports of remote worlds, the state of his income fluctuating between heady prosperity and a condition trembling between privation and destitution. At these times, occasionally, Maihac and Tarr would resort to occupations which were less than dignified, or even extra-legal.

During one of these latter periods they arrived at Mibbs on the world Gadron with a cargo of inexpensive power tools, whose consignee, at Port Merry on the world Praekops, at the back of Ursa Minor, had gone bankrupt. Freight charges, storage fees, port tax, imposts and duties totaled more than the value of the goods themselves, so that delivery of the cargo was refused, and the *Distilcord* was permitted four hours to be off-planet.

At Mibbs, local buyers came to the spaceport and looked over the merchandise. Neither Maihac nor Tarr were able to interpret the signals of the local merchants. Their slow and lethargic manner indicated profound indifference. Still, Maihac and Tarr thought that two merchants conferring in whispers, indicated a conspiracy to buy if they could be whipsawed down to a give-away price. So the two waited for the casual offers, but instead the merchants merely walked away. One of the buyers told Maihac: "This merchandise is of no value here, but you might sell it on consignment to Lorquin Shipping. They often will handle such stuff as this. But do not expect a fancy price."

Maihac approached the clerk at Lorquin Shipping Agency, who offered a nominal price for the merchandise. Maihac indignantly stalked out and crossed the road to Primrose Consolidators, where a portly young clerk named Yamb informed him that Lorquin freighted the material to Maz, where they sold at an artificially high price.

"In that case," said Maihac, "I will take the cargo to Maz and sell it myself."

"Very risky," said Yamb.

"Bah!" said Tarr cheerfully. "We are accustomed to risk."

Yamb shrugged. "You know your own capabilities best."

"It was clear that the factor Asrubal was mulcting the Houses of Romarth, who were too dignified to demand an accounting. I took the *Distilcord* to Maz. Local law prohibited landing except at the designated port of entry: a place called Amphol, at a most inconvenient distance from Romarth. It was here at Amphol, so I was told, that I must secure an import license."

Maihac landed the *Distilcord* at Amphol, which was little more than a cluster of sheds and warehouses in the middle of a bleak plain. Unsympathetic officials assured Maihac that import licenses were available only at Romarth, and probably not even there, since Lorquin Shipping dealt adequately with all needs.

Access to Romarth was not simple. Maihac was forbidden to use the ship's flitter, since such transport might serve to cheat the Loclor of what they considered their rightful tolls. Much less would Maihac be allowed to fly the *Distilcord* itself to Romarth, for the same reason. The usage of thousands of years had solidified the custom.

Leaving his mate Evan Tarr with the *Distilcord*, Maihac joined a convoy of cargo carriers across the plain. They were halted by a contingent of Loclor: tribesmen of the steppes, universally feared for their horrifying cruelty. They collected their tolls and the caravan proceeded. The next day another band of Loclor appeared and collected another toll, which was paid without demur. Maihac was told that if anyone protested, he was taken away, that he might 'dance with the girls', by the light of the twin moons.

At Rivermarsh Road they shifted to long barges and glided into the forest. For three days the barges moved quietly in the shade of tall trees: black yews, black-green larches and hemlocks of great age, mixed with local vegetation. At times they passed ruined mansions built of polished white stone, surrounded by decaying gardens; occasionally the houses were occupied; Maihac caught glimpses of the residents: in their gardens and along the terraces of their palatial homes. They were a handsome folk, graceful if somewhat formal in their mannerisms; obviously both wealthy and highly civilized. They moved with the easy langour of persons enjoying their leisure and the quiet of the forest.

The barges arrived at Romarth — a city of a thousand white palaces, only half of which were occupied, the others in various stages of dilapidation.

Dain Maihac made himself known to the appropriate persons and stated his reasons for coming to Romarth. He described himself as a merchant who wished to provide better service for the folk of Romarth at a quarter of the price they had been paying Lorquin Shipping Agency.

Maihac's proposal prompted a storm of controversy. A colloquy was ordered. The folk of Romarth were associated with about a hundred septs, each linked to many of the others by traditional ties of fealty, friendship, lineage or the untranslatable quality 'estaing'*.

Asrubal, of Hoy House, declared that he had taken the thankless supervision of Lorquin Agency upon himself as a public service. He stated that it was beneath his dignity to answer the charges, which in any case impugned his honour. He demanded that the interloper be expelled forthwith, and if the Loclor captured him on his return to Amphol, so much the better. As for the loose talk about prices, Asrubal had nothing to say: obviously! The clerks at Lorquin were responsible for such matters.

Asrubal made an imposing spectacle. He was not a handsome man. His torso was spare, his arms long and heavy. His long thick neck was as wide as his head, which was like a triangular knob of bone, from which dangled lank strands of black hair.

---

* Estaing: the closest approximation is 'honour', though 'estaing' is more susceptible to exact quantification. The concept supersedes 'shame', 'humiliation'; these affections are translated by 'estaing' into 'anger, mortification, annoyance'. Wrongs and affronts must be measured in terms of 'estaing', an exact equilibrium defined and imposed.

Maihac noticed that many of those present were not sympathetic to either Asrubal or Hoy House; there were at least two factions present at the colloquy, but the ramifications were too complex for his perceptions.

Asrubal's denunciation had annoyed Maihac, and he responded that Asrubal's control of Lorquin Shipping went beyond simple oversight. Asrubal had demonstrably been engaging in peculation; however, said Maihac, his purpose was not to expose Asrubal, but simply to secure an import license and to arrange for landing his ship at Romarth, rather than Amphol. Still, if necessary, his assertions were susceptible to proof, since in his possession were a large number of invoices inscribed by Asrubal personally, dictating the enormous markups to be levied upon the goods.

A number of persons were impressed by Maihac's statements. When Asrubal of Hoy stated that it was below the general estaing to haggle about prices like avaricious Shimshimaeans, the others said that in this case the defalcations, if they could be proved to exist, transcended haggling and if indeed they had been swindled, then their estaing must become involved in a very real sense; after all, while they were cavaliers of Romarth, they were not fools.

Again Maihac petitioned that he be allowed to bring the *Distilcord* to Romarth, rather than discharge cargo at Amphol. Asrubal of Hoy declared that it was the age-old tradition and had worked well until now; and that in any event the Loclor demanded their tolls. Maihac said that a few armed men could easily control the Loclor. Maihac was informed that for thousands of years the Roum had maintained an embargo upon modern weapons, from the certitude that they would fall into the hands of not only the Loclor, but others, equally dangerous and more difficult to control. Later, Maihac would learn that the creatures so described were the so-called 'white' house-ghouls.

The Council adjourned, so that the matter could be taken under consideration. Asrubal returned to Mibbs. Marit of Nol lodged Maihac in his palace: a place splendid beyond Maihac's previous experience. The servants were a slender pale race, silent, obedient, blank-faced, with delicate features and glossy black hair. According to Marit, they had been bred to their tasks ten thousand years previously, and now lacked the capacity for any other occupation. They were generated and nourished through infancy in a creche in the Old Quarter of Romarth. Agricultural work also was performed by such servants; the Loclor in general ignored them, as too contemptible to be noticed, but they often were the prey of the house-ghouls from whom they must be protected, since they were unable to defend themselves, such potentialities having been pruned from their genes.

A week passed. Maihac met Jamile of the House of Sadaj. She lived in a splendid palace with her grandparents; she was the last of the line: there were no more Sadaj. Jamile was unlike most Roum in that she was dissatisfied with her life, which she considered stagnant. She mentioned that the population of Romarth had been slowly declining from generation to generation; that others were also affected by a malaise. Three days later, Maihac, greatly daring and wondering at his own temerity, asked Jamile to marry him. She consented; they were married at once.

Time passed, during which Maihac thought that nothing was being done to further his case; Jamile assured him otherwise. "Litigation at Romarth is slow and tedious, especially when one of the parties at issue wills it so."

From Amphol came news that Asrubal had suddenly appeared, seized the *Distilcord* and had flown off into space with the ship and all its cargo. No word of Evan Tarr.

Maihac instantly complained to the City Council. When Asrubal at last returned and faced the accusation, instead of denial, he defended himself on the grounds that Maihac and Tarr had contravened traditional laws.

Maihac and the faction which supported him derided the defense and demanded quick retribution: Asrubal must be punished for his crimes and proper compensation paid to Maihac. The House of Hoy resisted the suggestion, and insisted upon a step-by-step examination of the issues, hoping to exhaust Maihac's patience or, better, find an opportunity to kill him. Evan Tarr had apparently escaped from Amphol in the flitter.

Time passed. Maihac learned much about Romarth. For all the elegance of its customs and the intricacy of its culture, it seemed an introverted archaism which had survived in isolation. The Roum knew little of the Gaean Reach; they assumed the folk of all other worlds to be coarse, brawling, indelicate, vulgar and insensitive. For a Roum, exquisitely trained in the social arts, exile to a far world seemed a harsh and lonely fate, where no one would appreciate or try to match his 'estaing'*.

The 'game' was the incessant interplay between the Roum, and was something between 'recreation' and 'obsession'. There were never formal winners, but everyone knew the champions and their relative status: sometimes a bitter-sweet triumph, for often had intricacies of the game resulted in tragedy — which only made the game more vivid. In any case, the Roum lived in a mood of subconscious melancholy. The population was declining, every year more of the ancient houses were surrendered, and every year the threat of their enemies became more immediate. The enemies were of two sorts. Most overt were the Loclor, who were cruel and unrelenting past calculation. Like the palace servants, they derived from early times. The first Roum had kept and worked a large number of slaves, whose characteristics they hoped to optimize through genetic alteration. Their efforts had borne unpredictable fruit. Some of the mutations had wasted away, or become grossly corpulent, and in either case useless at physical labor; others had created complicated systems of mental instability for themselves, making glories of pain and intransigence. They screamed, fought, climbed fences and fled out upon the steppes, where the strongest and most merciless survived, and in due course became the Loclor. Still others of the altered slaves, the most grotesque of the lot, crept away into the forest and hid in the far glens of Gomar Bastion. Thousands of years later the descendants of these secret people began to slip into deserted palaces and occupy them; they became known as the white house-ghouls: by reason of their macabre habits. In recent times they had dared enter Romarth itself, occupying old palaces on the outskirts of the city, then others ever closer to the center plaza. From time to time a band of cavaliers might undertake to clear an old mansion of

---

* Estaing: essentially, the traits and skills by which one's place in society was established. There were many components, including flair, grace, perfect ritual courtesy, impassive bravery, and much else. Estaing was an essential adjunct to one who wished to play the 'game'.

the creatures, but often the cost in human life was high, and to what end? No one wished to live in the house after it had been cleared, since the house-ghouls always returned, to reclaim what they had once won.

All this and much else Dain Maihac learned as he waited. Time moved slowly at Romarth; the concept of squeezing a maximum advantage from each passing instant was alien to the Roum mentality. In the course of the 'game' there were always more than enough fascinations and distractions to accommodate them: flirtation, lovemaking and the endless permutations of the erotic process as developed at Romarth after ten thousand years of refinement.

Meanwhile Jamile became pregnant.

Maihac understood that bitter opposition from Hoy House had been thwarting him. He seized the opportunity of a high-level colloquy and brought matters to a head. He displayed a price list issued by Asrubal and declared that these prices were inflated five times, that he himself could supply the same goods at a fraction of the cost.

The remarks stunned the colloquy. In the first place, they were harsh, realistic and insulting to Asrubal and the House of Hoy.

Asrubal said with great control: "You wilfully distort the truth. In short, you are a liar, of the most vicious sort. The facts are these: I collect a modest profit, sufficient to maintain operation, but no more."

"In that case," said Maihac, "all is well. You shall buy from me, at eighty percent of your previous costs, and make double your previous profit. I will perform the dangerous and back-breaking tasks incident to the work, and attempt somehow to scratch out a profit, and all will be satisfied. There is no need for further discussion."

Asrubal refused to commit himself to the plan, and described Maihac as a 'cunning off-world trickster, whom we would be wise to extirpate.'

The remarks were adjudged intemperate and caused further delay. Jamile's time arrived and she gave birth to twins: Jaro and Garlet.

At last, after two years, the consensus found against Asrubal; he was censured and enjoined against future peculation. Further, he was required to make compensation to Maihac for the *Distilcord* and its lost cargo.

Asrubal's exaggerated estaing prompted him to a cold and metallic indifference to the force of the judgment; he turned and stalked from the chamber. His contumacy surprised no one, nor did any of his peers become exercised. After ten thousand years of quarrels and accommodations, methods for dealing with almost any situation had been devised.

Nonetheless, events moved slowly at Romarth and six months passed before the Maihacs were tendered a draught upon the Hoy House account, at the Natural Bank of Mibbs, to the sum of three hundred thousand sols.

A sense of crisis hung in the air. Maihac had been warned that he went in imminent danger of assassination.

The time had come to leave Romarth. Evan Tarr brought the flitter from its hiding place to a rendezvous in the garden of the ancient Holderness Palace. Maihac, Jamile and the two children arrived by secret ways; the flitter awaited them; escape was at hand. But they had been betrayed. Dark shapes entered the garden; at the back stood Asrubal. Evan Tarr was killed in the fighting, while Maihac bundled Jamile and his children aboard the flitter. For a moment he thought to be overwhelmed; then he kicked, slashed, thrust, struck and won free. He took the flitter careening into the air, and it seemed that they had escaped. Then Jamile discovered that only one of her children was aboard the flitter; the second had been snatched out. Maihac brought the flitter back in a tight circle. They looked down into the faces of their enemies. Asrubal stood holding aloft in savage triumph the child. It was Garlet. He kicked and squirmed, and struck Asrubal in the face, prompting Asrubal to dash the child down into a clutter of stones, so that Jamile gave up the boy for dead.

Maihac flew Jamile and Jaro to Amphol and put them aboard a passenger packet for the voyage to Mibbs. Maihac turned the flitter back toward Romarth. Were Garlet still alive, no matter how tenuously, Maihac would try to rescue him. If not, he would exact vengeance.

Maihac's plans failed. As he boarded the flitter, he was captured by a passing band of Loclor and carried off into the steppe.

Now for Maihac began an eventful three years. He remained alive partly through luck, partly through his own capabilities and partly through his will to live. First, for the amusement of his captors, he danced with the girls and killed nine. The Loclor found this feat amusing, and conceived new ways to torment Maihac hoping to make him cry out in pain. "Had I done so, they might have tired of the sport and killed me at once. I developed stoicism and so I survived the grace period during which they became accustomed to me and my peculiar habits. The Loclor are not nice. They have no redeeming qualities. If they have any rudimental moral system, it is unknown to me."

Skirl shuddered. "The experience must have changed you greatly."

"So I suppose," said Maihac. "But no matter; I am as I am." He returned to his story. At one time he became aware that the young bucks were planning to fall on him en masse and kill him for practice. To forestall them, Maihac challenged a sub-chief, to the general aston-ishment. "If you are beaten, then we boil your head," he was told.

"And if I win?"

"You will not win!"

"If I win, I keep my life?"

"Just as you like." The concession was made indifferently, and Maihac knew that it meant little, since the Loclor honored no inconve-nient contracts. Nevertheless he fought with the subchief by firelight. The occasion, as he recalled it, was colorful and dramatic. The two moons were set; the sky showed a million far galaxies: wisps of pale light, puffs of starlit jelly. The Loclor males wore breeches of dark scar-let, saffron, pale blue; the wide flaring legs were embroidered with crude floriations of black iron wire. Loclor skin was like leather the color of corroded bronze, occasionally showing a maroon luster, as at the cheekbones and along the shoulders of the men. Many of the females, for reasons never made clear to Maihac, stained their faces pasty white; they wore conical leather hats with ear-flaps slanting away from their heads. Corselets of thongs and beads hung from their shoul-ders terminating in billowing skirts of black leather. Men and women alike stood a head taller than the ordinary man, with short necks, heavy heads with large features which seemed contorted and twisted to the middle of the faces.

The contest began. It was to consist of a complicated game involving piles of stones and transferring them to new stations while trying to disable the opponent. Maihac was led into a ring formed by a circle of fires and told to wait while the stones were counted: a slow process of incredible ineptitude. As he waited, naked children darted at him and thrust burning twigs against his legs, until he caught up one and threw it into the nearest fire. It howled and ran to the back of the crowd where it was cuffed and kicked and told to be silent; meanwhile the other children desisted from their mischief.

The bout began. Maihac had only his wits and his quickness to aid him. His opponent moved stones at will; when Maihac tried to do the same, he was chased and pressed so hard that he dropped his stones, to the general amusement. The sub-chief pointed: "There you see it! The great kettle yonder! I need move ten more stones, and then we boil your head."

"Not just yet," said Maihac. With desperate effort he flung a stone into the face of his antagonist; the sub-chief dropped, with his facial processes crushed; Maihac transferred the stones and was silently conceded victory. The forefinger claw of the sub-chief had furrowed his face; this wound produced his first scar.

Two days later a warrior named Koras approached and compared Maihac to a pestilential rodent. "Now your life will end."

"But I was guaranteed my life!"

"Not by me." Koras reached for his axe with the six-foot haft; Maihac caught him off-balance and toppled him to the ground. He took Koras's cutlass and held it to the corded red throat. "I don't want to kill you — because there would only be more to kill. I want you for my ally, who protects me. Do you agree to serve me in this way?"

Koras could not understand what was required of him, but after Maihac explained Koras, surprised and perplexed, agreed. "I submit! I name you kinsman." Maihac stood aside. Koras jumped up and flung himself upon Maihac, intending to tear him apart. His claws raked Maihac's face. Maihac crouched, cut Koras's heavy hamstrings; the great form staggered, toppled. Again Maihac pressed the cutlass against Koras's neck. "Give me your pledge!"

Koras muttered: "Yes, yes; it was a great mistake; you have dealt me a terrible wound. I want no more."

Maihac moved aside. Koras hunched painfully erect, then roared in jubilation: "Still, wound or not, I shall kill you!"

But Koras was now unsteady; Maihac cut at the back of the right ankle; with a groan of resignation Koras again fell. He cried out: "This time I swear by my axe-brothers; may they smother in ordure if I break faith; by the drip from the garden of the Mekli!"

"This time he means it," said the bystanders, who had been watching, grimly amused.

Maihac stood aside. Koras, using his axe as a cane, heaved himself up, to stand on half-severed ankles. He looked at Maihac. "Now it is your turn. "

After a furious struggle, Maihac was able, first, to hack away Koras's right arm, then finally kill him.

The bystanders muttered and exchanged critical opinions. One said to Maihac: "Why did you toy with him so long?"

"It was a whim," said Maihac. "I thought he might help me stay alive."

"What foolishness! You will live only until someone feels in the mood to split your head."

Maihac made himself useful by repairing motor wagons, and was no longer constantly in danger of attack. He was not sure of his status, but eventually decided that he was regarded as a low-caste member of the tribe.

Young Loclor bucks constantly engaged each other in a wild and dangerous form of wrestling, into which Maihac was often drawn for lack of better adversary; if he tried to avoid the sport he was mercilessly kicked back and forth and prodded, until in desperation he exerted himself, which usually won him further bruises and sprains, but no sympathy — this, like other projective emotions, being alien to the Loclor psyche. For the sake of survival he applied himself not to avoiding the conflict, but to excelling in it, and refining the techniques of which he was already familiar.

There were few modern weapons on Maz; the Loclor used long-hafted axes and heavy swords and occasionally carried a cutlass. These weapons were too heavy for Maihac. He carried a cutlass, a hatchet and contrived a small cross-bow with an effective range of a hundred feet, which he kept hidden from the tribesmen.

The Loclor band wandered far afield, to the far side of the continent. Maihac was not sure what might happen if he tried to go his own way. He suspected that he would be hunted down and killed for no other reason than idle malice. Now it made no great difference, since he could not hope to survive a solitary journey to Amphol.

Time passed: months, a year, two years. Maihac, driven by circumstances, assimilated many of the harsh attitudes of the Loclor; he became someone whom, as his former self, he would not have recognized. The tribe wandered north, occasionally meeting other tribes. When this occurred, there might be formal salutes, and a ritual exchange of females. Occasionally challenges might be issued, and a champion from each tribe engaged themselves in a duel by firelight. Once, to his intense surprise, Maihac was with saturnine humor pushed forward into the ring and required to fight as the tribe's champion. Maihac, profiting by his experience, far quicker and more agile than his opponent, managed to win the bout, though suffering a terrible wound in the process, which the women of the tribe matter-of-factly set to rights. He was neither congratulated nor given any recognition whatever for his victory; he had won, the drama was over, the deed was in the past and had no bearing upon the future.

The tribe moved slowly to the southwest and came to a great river, which they dared not cross, since none could swim. They followed the river south, into a gloomy forest of tall conifers. After several days travel they came upon the abandoned white palaces of a ruined city. The Loclor long before had claimed one of these as their own; now they found white house-ghouls stirring in the shadows. The infestation aroused the Loclor to a fury. They lit torches and set out to purge the palace of its infestation, and the house-ghouls melted away before them, uttering peevish outcries but offering no resistance.

They were gone, or so it seemed, leaving only a rank odor behind. Maihac went to examine the frescos in what had been a grand salon. He heard a soft sound; turning, he found a house-ghoul near at hand, pointing a long crooked arm toward him as if in woeful accusation. Maihac stood frozen; the house-ghoul, leering, reached out to grasp him; Maihac struck away the arm. The house-ghoul screamed and with a great flutter of its robes sprang upon Maihac, who was saved by his reflexes alone. He rolled aside, and found himself engaged in the most terrible battle of his life, with the house-ghoul maintaining a constant screaming, imploring in a melodious voice. The creature at last became still, sprawled across Maihac, whose face had been torn open and scalp ripped away. A number of Loclor had been watching; now they turned away, Maihac realized that they took him for dead.

2.

The house was quiet. The Loclor were gone. Maihac knew the house-ghouls would be back. He crawled to the front of the palace, and looked up and down the river. He stared in wonder. The large building on the river-bank — could that be the creche? Was this city Romarth? He staggered along the river and presently met a group of cavaliers. They took him to the House of Sadaj, where he was tended as best could be done. Nevertheless, his face was a terrible caricature of its old self; when he looked in a mirror he was unrecognizable. So be it, he thought, at least for the moment.

Asrubal was not at hand. Maihac tried to learn Garlet's fate, and was told that Asrubal had killed the infant.

Maihac returned to Amphol, where he took passage to Mibbs aboard the passenger packet. At Mibbs Aubert Yamb informed him that Asrubal had come to Mibbs, then had travelled onward — where he could not say.

At the spaceport Maihac learned that Asrubal had taken passage to the world Kammerwelt. Maihac did the same and after a week made a connection. When he arrived at Kammerwelt he traced Asrubal to Point Extase. He also learned of the woman drowning and the missing small boy, also presumed drowned. The landlord mentioned the missing boat; Maihac inquired downstream for any news of Jaro, and finally heard of the boy brought to the hospital by the Faths. The attendants mentioned that the Faths had spoken of adopting the waif; Maihac went to the Department of Vital Statistics and learned the Faths' address on Gallingale. He managed to distract the clerk's attention and excised the Faths' name and address from the files.

Maihac travelled to Thanet on Gallingale, using the identity of his old chief mate Evan Tarr. There he learned that the Faths had provided a very good home for Jaro; reluctantly he decided to wait until Jaro had reached maturity before making himself known.

It so happened that Jaro had made his own choices, without Maihac's intervention, and Maihac now felt uncomfortable with the need for revealing his identity. He temporized, thinking that by some miracle it might not be necessary.

"And that is the story," Maihac told Jaro and Skirl.

"First: the bank draught," said Jaro. "We should make sure of the money."

Skirl said impassively: "You will also call Asrubal's attention to yourself."

"I hope to do more than that."

Skirl compressed her mouth. "I understand your motivations, but I think you should calculate pros and cons very carefully. You cannot enjoy revenge if you are dead."

"I agree, and I don't want to be dead."

* * * * * *

The executive officer at the Natural Bank was reluctant so much as to touch the draft. Maihac told him: "The draught is a legitimate instrument, made out to my order. Here is my identification. If you refuse to pay to my legitimate demand, I shall instantly call in the Economic Regulation Arm of the IPCC, and I will call for punitive damages. The IPCC will levy a further charge upon you. You owe me approximately three hundred thousand sols at six percent compound interest for almost fifteen years. This amounts to about seven hundred and fifty thousand sols. Pay me now or I go to the IPCC. A bank draught will be satisfactory."

"That is Hoy money!" protested the banker. "It is a draught upon their primary fund! They will be perplexed, why, after all these years —"

In the end the banker paid over bearer notes to the stipulated amount, which Maihac immediately took to the offices of the Allardyce Bank of Mibbs, and deposited to the account of 'Jaro and/or Dain Maihac'.

The three returned to the *Pharsang*, and studied maps of Maz. Skirl lacked all enthusiasm for proceeding further. "You have found your father and mother," she told Jaro. "You have acquired this ship and a great deal of money; if you go to Maz you risk it all, and why? To take revenge upon Asrubal? Is it worth the risk? You have already taken his money, and he has been dishonored."

Dain Maihac looked at Jaro. "What she says is true."

Jaro asked: "And what of you?"

"I will return to Maz."

"I will come with you."

Skirl protested angrily: "It is childish bravado!" She addressed Maihac. "Have you not suffered enough pain and mutilation?"

"More than enough. Still — I must go."

Skirl turned upon Jaro. "And what of you? There are no real reasons forcing you to Maz."

Jaro pondered a moment, then said: "There are three reasons. The first is Dain Maihac. The second is Asrubal."

"And the third?"

"I don't know who or what it is, or even if it is anything more than a voice talking to me from the back to my brain."

"It is the soul of your dead brother. His name was Garlet."

"It may be so. All this has nothing to do with you, in any case. Why not return to Gallingale on a passenger ship? We'll share the money with you; there is more than enough for all of us."

The suggestion failed to please Skirl, and she sat scowling, lips compressed. She said: "For a fact, I am curious regarding Maz, and I would like to visit Romarth. I know that there is danger, but it will not be like before, and in any case I am willing to risk it."

"There will be less danger, for a fact," said Maihac. "On this occasion we will be prepared."

Chapter 7

1.

The *Pharsang* departed Gadron and crossed space to the world Olanche. At the industrial complex Rocamadour, the No. 2 flitter was converted into a small gunboat, while the *Pharsang* itself was fitted with weapons, both long and short range, and much other equipment not ordinarily found aboard a commercial ship unless that ship were being fitted out for illicit enterprises.

During the conversion, Skirl spent much time exploring the Municipal Gardens, the Mile-deep Pit, and the peculiar little enclave inhabited principally by the yellow-robed Fo Credence. One day Jaro found her sitting alone at a cafe in the Central Market watching the folk of the city. He asked politely if he might join her and received a shrug which he interpreted as acquiescence, though he could not be sure. Skirl had become a mystery to him. When he tried to divine her moods, using standard methods, he received contradictory signals, so that sometimes she seemed almost unfriendly. As the days passed, the dark moods became more frequent, or perhaps Jaro had become more sensitive to their comings and goings. Like every other aspect of Skirl, they were unpredictable, though Jaro had come to suspect that they were provoked by Dain Maihac, rather than other causes, such as himself. The reason might not be absolutely abstruse, thought Jaro; Maihac, though unfailingly polite, was unmoved by her whims.

Jaro studied the pretty, delicate, if rather sullen, features covertly. After a moment she asked: "Why are you staring at me with such perturbation?"

Jaro said evenly: "If you must know, I was thinking of the first time I saw you, when you marched into the schoolroom and took command."

Skirl smiled. "What did you think of me?"

"I thought you fascinating beyond words. I wanted to sweep you up and carry you away to some remote wonderworld where you would recognize my own magnificence and fall helplessly in love with me." Jaro grimaced. "I never dared so much as lay a finger on you. I doubt if you so much as noticed me."

"Ha!" said Skirl. "You would be surprised to learn what goes on in a young girl's mind."

"Hm." Jaro digested the information.

"But I did. I saw a nice-looking boy, clean, intelligent, but also rather dreamy. At the time I was angry with my father, my mother, the school, all of Thanet, and even the Clam Muffins, and I lacked sympathy for boys with poetic temperaments, no matter how wistful their yearnings."

Jaro smiled sadly. "I was quite young. I was afraid that you would —" his voice trailed off.

"That I would do what?"

"Scorn me; hold me up to humiliation."

Skirl studied him under level eyebrows. "That was a real possibility, very profound."

Jaro shrugged. "You've given me very little encouragement."

"Oh? I came to your house to live with you. I followed you aboard the *Pharsang*, and I am here now at Rocamadour. These are broad hints."

Jaro turned to look off across the marketplace. When he turned back, he found that Skirl had risen to her feet and was standing close beside him.

"I am Skirl Hutsenreiter. I am unique, a Clam Muffin, a creature of fable, desirable beyond words, charged with glory, like Erlu of the Seven Dawns."

Jaro stared in wonderment.

Skirl asked: "What do you see?"

"You are as you say you are! It is magic indeed!"

Skirl held out her hands. Jaro took them. She asked: "Do you feel my touch?"

Jaro nodded. "Your fingers are warm and strong; they seem to pulse."

Skirl stepped close to him. Their bodies were in contact and her face was only inches from his. "Do you know that I am here?" asked Skirl.

Jaro answered in a husky voice: "I know very well where you are."

"Kiss me."

Jaro obeyed the instruction. "Think!" said Skirl, "you might have done that long ago."

"No matter; we'll do it now, and perhaps get up to speed."

Skirl shook her head and drew back. "That was the first time I have kissed you, and it may well be the last. The time has come and gone for kissing."

Jaro stared at her blankly. "I don't understand." But Skirl was already walking away from him. "Wait!" cried Jaro. "Why are you so impetuous, especially when you have just told me of my mistakes?"

Skirl paused and looked over her shoulder. "What mistakes are you talking about?"

"I should never have been afraid of you," declared Jaro. "That is clear to me, and I see how easy it is to love you."

Skirl nodded. "This may be true, but still we must be careful. Love is like a formal dance; the partners must dance the same steps to the same music; otherwise they make themselves ridiculous, capering and jumping like clowns at the carnival."

"Just so," said Jaro doubtfully. "Of course, I am not much of a dancer —"

"No matter. I will show you the proper steps, and we will select the proper music, but it must be our own private, personal music: soft and quiet. It can't be Dain Maihac's songs of fury and revenge and hatred."

Jaro grimaced, enlightened at last. "Before I can sing so much as a note, I need to clear away the noise in my head. This is why I must go to Romarth."

Skirl's mouth drooped. "Let Maihac go, if he is a mind to do so; we will wait here."

Jaro shook his head. "I could never do such a thing. If you like, you can return to Thanet with all the money you want, and I will join you as soon as possible."

"And I should wait for you, month after month, year after year, as Jamile waited for Dain Maihac, who showed up fifteen years too late with a face like a fright-mask?"

Jaro had nothing to say; somberly the two returned to the *Pharsang*.

Here Jaro tried to kiss her; she made no resistance, but it was like kissing a stone.

2.

The *Pharsang* departed Olanche and set off on a course up and out, toward the brink of nothingness. Fringe stars appeared and drifted astern. The Yellow Rose Star slid past off the port beam, slightly below horizontal. Far ahead the luminous smudges of other galaxies showed against the black.

At last, still a vast distance, a spark marked the position of a lonely lost star: Nightlamp.

The HANDBOOK OF THE PLANETS made no mention of Maz, nor did any of the usual references. The single item of information was a rather rough map supplied by Aubert Yamb.

---:O:---

Maz was a world slightly smaller than Earth. One face of the world was covered by ocean. A pair of small mountainous continents were buried under glaciers; a third large continent, ungainly and irregular, sprawled across both temperate zones and the intervening equatorial strip. The physiography included every sort of landscape: deserts, swamps, grasslands, high savannahs, mountains old and new. A great central forest was traversed by several rivers; surrounding were wide steppes, broken only by a few low hills. At the center of the forest, on a loop of the Sallou River, Yamb had located 'Romarth'; north of the forest was the spaceport Amphol. A notation indicated that 'Travellers bound for Romarth might proceed only after making local arrangements.'

The voyage proceeded. Maz became visible, then grew to become an object with identifiable surface features. A vast forest shrouded the cool highlands to the south. Elsewhere the terrain was wild and rugged, but for the most part steppe.

The *Pharsang* descended. On the landing field at Amphol rested a cargo vessel of medium size; the macroscope revealed it to be the Lorquin Agency's *Canmech*, now in the process of discharging cargo.

The time was late afternoon. Maihac put the *Pharsang* into station five miles above the space terminal. They waited while the sun Nightlamp set in a flare of melancholy colors. One of the moons climbed the sky, followed by the other. They glowed soft and winsome, like pearls in milk.

Jaro and Maihac descended in the armed flitter. They landed among sand dunes behind the space terminal and approached the *Canmech* through the darkness. No one was astir. Maihac forced the entry port and worked invisible mischief upon the codes in the control matrices, effectively putting the *Canmech* out of commission. "Asrubal can hide but he can't escape. He is marooned on Maz."

The two returned toward the flitter. At the murmur of low voices, they stopped short, to discover that a troop of warriors, wandering by night, had come upon the flitter. The discovery excited them, and caused them to make odd shrill noises. Jaro studied them in wonder; could these be human beings, derived from ordinary Gaean stock? Maihac seemed to read his mind. "They are mutations — partly natural, partly biogenetic freaks."

Jaro studied the creatures with awe. In synchrony with their breathing the black tongues darted in and out of their mouths, lending the faces a flickering vivacity.

Maihac whispered: "Notice the fangs! These are 'Long-tooth' Loclors; I was with a different clan."

The two were noticed; the alarm was sounded: a wild exultant ululation that prickled the hairs on Jaro's neck. His muscles became limp and nerveless and his jaw sagged. He had no time for horrified thoughts. The Loclor came at a crouching run, faces moonlit. Jaro's hand shook as he aimed his gun. Maihac was steadier, and in the end a dozen bodies lay on the moonlit sand.

Jaro stared down at the awesome corpses, and looked with respect at the man with the scarred face: his father.

The two returned aloft to the *Pharsang*. where Skirl pretended indifference in their exploits. "What next?"

"We make ourselves known at Romarth."

"And then?"

"We see what happens along the way."

"Hmmf," said Skirl disapprovingly. "That seems a most precarious plan."

"You are no doubt right, but I can't think of anything better."

"And how do I figure into your scheme?"

"Someone must stay aboard the ship, to deal with emergencies."

"And I am that 'someone'?"

"Only for a time," said Maihac soothingly.

Skirl shrugged. "Just as you like."

Throughout the night the *Pharsang* drifted over the forest, following the course of the River Sallou; at dawn the city Romarth spread below: a great pattern of boulevards, white palaces and dank dark gardens.

The *Pharsang* hovered at a height of five miles. Dain Maihac identified the several districts. The Sallou divided the city roughly into half; to the north and west the Roum maintained their ancient mode of existence, with retinues of servants attentive to their desires. To the south the palaces gradually ceased to be inhabited and many had lapsed into dilapidation. The house-ghouls had taken a de facto, if desultory and irregular, possession of the deserted palaces. Though abhorred by the Roum, they were tolerated, since they prevented the Loclor from occupation.

The boulevards of Romarth converged upon a central plaza, surrounded by a number of public buildings, with functions which long since had lost their meaning and now were ceremonial only. Maihac described them to the best of his recollection. He said: "Notice that long building downriver from the plaza: the structure with the three low domes? The Roum call this place the 'Creche'; it is where the servants are bred, matured and trained. During early times the genetic scientists attempted to create a variety of service specialists."

Skirl was puzzled. "What does that mean?"

"Different physical types adapted to the best performance of specific functions. They thought of themselves as idealists and visionaries, but their theories failed since most of their creations were unable to procreate. The exceptions were the creatures who developed into the various strains of Loclor and house-ghouls. The servants could not procreate, but they were easy to produce from matrix protoplasm, which is stored at the Creche."

Skirl asked: "Do the Roum ever travel about the Reach?"

"The Roum lack interest in other places, which they believe to be morasses of vulgarity, dirt, bad smells, sour food and enforced intimacy with strangers."

"That is a fair statement," said Skirl. "Still, it is not very adventurous."

"They also have a rather lofty prejudice against offworlders. Jamile, after she met me, developed a cultural claustrophobia, or something of the sort, and was anxious to leave, but she was the exception. As for adventure, the Roum find all they need at home. Passions are intense. They fight duels for trivial causes, attended by surging music; the duels are halfway between high drama and a struggle for prestige.

"Still, the Roum are neither ignoble nor laughable; in general, they are amusing, gracious, and extremely urbane."

Skirl shuddered. "They seem like posturing dolls."

Maihac agreed. "Without their servants they would never survive. They might not even know how to undress themselves."

The three discussed circumstances and optimum strategies. Skirl took only a small part in the conversations, since she still resented her passive role in the forthcoming venture.

The group at last settled upon a procedure which had, at the very least, the virtue of simplicity.

The afternoon waned; the two men dressed in garments similar to those worn by the Roum.

The sun sank into the forest; shadows fell across the ancient boulevards. Maihac and Jaro descended to the city in the armed flitter. They landed in the shadows at the back of the Sadaj palace. Maihac went off alone, leaving Jaro to guard the flitter.

An hour passed. Maihac and a middle-aged man returned; Jaro was introduced to Chan Sadaj, his great-uncle by reason of a complicated relationship. The three concealed the flitter, then entered the palace, where Jaro was bemused by the splendour of the grand chambers and their appointments refined and perfected across thousands of years. Servants moved quietly through the shadows: slight supple creatures with still faces. They wore tight grey trousers, dark green tabards embroidered in purple and gray. Jaro inspected them with interest. Their skins were pale; their hair rose above their heads in a flexible peak, like a candle-flame.*

Maihac and Jaro conferred with the grandees of Sadaj House. They learned that Asrubal was currently resident at Hoy House. He had never regained the full scope of his former status, but still exerted influence at Hoy House.

---

* Certain of the servants, of the highest caste, received special training and became skillful at special tasks, such as cooking, household management, metal fabrication, and other crafts. In general, even the high castes lacked initiative. They also lacked humor; all were imbued with an organic distaste, even horror, of causing pain or injury — a trait built into their psyches by the early bio-geneticists. Their sexual organs were atrophied, thus the necessity for reproduction by way of the forcing vats in the Creche.

Chapter 8

1.

Historically, Romarth had been ruled by factions, in a fluid ever-changing alteration of interests and loyalties. At the moment two factions were preeminent: the Blues, dominated by Sadaj House and Fierl House, and the Greens, which included Hoy House. The appearance of Maihac and Jaro stirred new eddies in the continuing flux of intrigue, plot, counterplot, danger! Asrubal was not only still extant, but he had regained much of his previous prestige. The two factions, the Blues and the Greens, debated the credibility not only of Asrubal, but also of Maihac and Jaro.

The charges against Asrubal had aroused neither surprise nor outrage — nothing but a muted distaste, as if the worst had already been accepted as a natural disaster, to which an accommodation must be made. In this context the accusers became the objects of resentment, rather than the accused. There was a disposition for temporizing, and careful study of the legal doctrines involved. To this the Sadaj sept made strong objections, but could not prevent a week's postponement before convocation of the judicial assembly.

Skirl had insisted upon descending to Romarth in the remaining flitter; the *Pharsang* drifted alone in the sky.

The cavaliers* of Romarth conducted themselves without notable warmth toward the three off-worlders; they were instinctively felt to be trouble-making outsiders, with no perception of the delicate control of existence as practised at Romarth.

---

* Cavalier: an approximate translation, more accurate in its overtones than 'young nobleman', 'knight', 'bravo', or any other such expression.

Skirl was told by a handsome cavalier: "We are cognizant of thirteen distinct sensory perceptions, some brave, others as pale as the memory of an old sachet. We orchestrate the fleeting instants of existence as an impresario conducts the musicians of his orchestra. Now then: do you believe me?"

"Of course! Why should I not?"

"Then come with me now, to my Gray and Lilac Chamber. My servants will disrobe you, and spray you head to toe with a crust. I shall appear, in my own crust, of a different tint and a different flavor. In the end you will find yourself floating in a warm pool on which there is a film of the stuff called Nanomei. After a time, the servants bring you out, lax and lethargic, on a white cushion. They dress you in linen fragrant with may, and once again we meet, to eat and to drink, and while away the afternoon. "

"That sounds nice," said Skirl.

"Good! Are you ready?"

"I don't think so. The chance doesn't come all that often, but — no." Skirl frowned and rubbed her nose. "No. Better not."

On the following day, for reasons beyond his understanding, Jaro was challenged to a duel by Huon, a frosty-faced cavalier from Farque House. Jaro accepted the challenge, if he were allowed the choice of weapons.

His enemy, a cavalier of the most ineffable elegance, shrugged disdainfully. "As you like."

Jaro chose four-foot staves.

Huon was shocked by the brutality of the concept. "It is the weapon of a vulgar animal." With a chilly smile Huon refused to link his proud name to so sordid an affair. If Jaro refused to fight like a gentleman, Huon would order his servants to strike him ten blows with a pussy-willow whip.

"Then you may use your sword and I will use the stave," said Jaro.

The two fought; Jaro broke Huon's wrist and his knee and threw his sword into the river, along with Huon's fine hat. "That is what I think of you and your ridiculous hat," said Jaro.

During the duel Jaro's inner voice had been silent; now Jaro became aware of a low sad rumble, like the sound of surf.

Jaro asked questions of the Sadaj's: Who was Garlet? What had happened to him? He was eventually told that Garlet had been snatched away from Jamile's servants by Asrubal. While Jamile was yet able to see, Asrubal threw the infant high in the air, so that it fell into a quarry of broken rocks, to dash out its brains.

2.

Asrubal refused to appear at the Justiciary, declaring that the action was a farce, hanging upon purported wrongs done to an off-world huckster, or perhaps those of his son — he, Asrubal, had not troubled to look into the complaint, but in any event it was below his dignity to set foot from Hoy House. Such being the case, the Justiciars, concealing their vexation, took themselves and the appurtenances of their justice to where it best suited Asrubal's convenience: to Hoy House.

Asrubal was accused of larceny, peculation, treachery, assault, murder and attempted murder. The charges were read by Tansett, the Hoy Magister: politely in a manner of strained distaste and polite incredulity, and languid disinterest, as if to insulate those present from such tiresome considerations, which even if true had far better be ignored and forgotten, so that everyone might return to other more entertaining matters.

Despite the boredom and disinterest, the business of the day proceeded. Evidence placing Asrubal at Point Ecstase was produced, together with an explicit identification of Asrubal from a photograph by Jamile's landlord, which linked Asrubal directly to the murder. Jamile's letter was read into the record. Its effect was hard to assess. Asrubal listened impassively.

The question of Asrubal's motives arose. Jaro pointed out that Asrubal was obviously anxious to recover his draft of three hundred thousand sols to Dain Maihac, which at that time had not yet been cashed. Jaro mentioned, almost incidentally, that the situation in this regard had changed; that only a short time ago the draft had been tendered for funding at the Natural Bank of Mibbs, where, after fifteen years, it had compounded to seven hundred and fifty thousand sols, which the Bank had charged to the Hoy House account.

The news brought consternation to the Hoys. They turned in shock upon Asrubal. "We are destitute, thanks to you!"

Asrubal, still stonily silent, stared at his shouting kinsmen. Their mood had altered; Asrubal had committed more than a simple peccadillo; he had brought a noble house to a condition of want and shame, and had extinguished the greater part of their estaing.

The sharpness of the mood transferred to those who had brought the charges. Elvil Hoy demanded of Dain Maihac that he refund the money. Maihac laughed. "Where were you when Asrubal robbed me and destroyed my ship?"

Elvil Hoy next addressed Jaro: "You accuse Asrubal, but your own actions lack all grace! There is no reason in your position: this is obvious! Your face is distorted with hatred; you live and breathe contention! Why do you do these things? Do you enjoy your malice?"

Jaro retorted: "If Asrubal had murdered your mother, your face would be distorted too!"

Tansett uttered a cold reproof. "Come now! We are prepared to hear well-documented facts, but please avoid lachrymose or maudlin sentiment."

"Certainly, sir," said Jaro, smiling grimly. "If you need further facts, they are at your disposal. So far as we are concerned, the case is firm."

Elvil Hoy stated: "We have heard serious charges. The accused has a right to reply, if he so desires."

"Bah!" said Asrubal scornfully. "What is there to reply to? They have brought you scandal and rumor, and everyone darts here and there in a panic! Where is probity? Where is balance? Where is simple justice? Must I, the accused, point it out for your instruction?"

"As you wish," said Elvil Hoy frostily. "It is your privilege to do so."

"Aye, then! That I will! These charges are no better than flatulence, of a particularly purulent sort.

"The premise to the case is the Lorquin franchise for commercial service to Maz. This firm and steady contract assures the Roum of the strong and steady service they have so long enjoyed, at most reasonable rates. The mountebank Maihac, through the tactic of underpricing stolen goods, tried to shake confidence in the integrity of Lorquin Shipping, and succeeded so well that the bemused Justiciars enforced an unjust fine of three hundred thousand sols upon me when through neglect he lost his ship and cargo to the Loclors.

"I appealed the verdict, but Maihac attempted to flee with his spouse and family. I protested strongly, and — in accordance with established practice, took into custody, to serve as surety for my money, a member of the family. Contrary to assertion, the child was not dashed upon the rocks; I tossed it down to one of my servants, with instructions to care for it until further notice."

Asrubal threw his long arms high, in dramatic emphasis. "Who is this skulker, this cheapjack Maihac who talks of honour? Our memories are long; who will think honour of Maihac who ran so fleetly from Romarth? Tansett, Glynstra, do you remember? How can you forget? The off-world trickster, running on pointed toes, knees jerking high — all the while ignoring the surety left behind: his own son! Eh then, Tansett: think of it! This is the man who so easily uses the word 'honour'!"

Tansett spoke dourly: "I know nothing of this; the matter is long past and dim down the stream of years."

Dain Maihac said: "I can clarify the subject of 'honour'. The evidence is on my face and elsewhere about my body. I went to Amphol to safeguard my wife and son, then I returned to reclaim what Asrubal calls his 'surety'. I was captured by the Loclors, by Asrubal's instruction. I survived three years. They left me for dead after I had killed a house-ghoul. This was fifteen years ago. Asrubal was gone off-world for his murdering. I was assured that my son Garlet was dead. I left Maz and traced my other son Jaro and found him on a world far away, and we are here to bring justice down upon Asrubal."

"His tale is patent fabrication!" declared Delfin Hoy, though without any great conviction. "These deeds are both strange and impossible!"

"Not so," said Arno Sadaj. "We found him fifteen years ago, at the edge of death and we saw the house-ghoul he had killed. He wore Loclor garments and with his scars and wounds he was more terrifying than any Loclor. His tale is true."

Asrubal sat motionless, face like a stone. Tansett spoke in a troubled voice: "We must at this instant resolve the matter of Asrubal's so-called 'surety'. He now claims that he did not kill this infant, so — where is it? Its value as surety is moot, and Asrubal cannot justify retention."

Arno Roybel said drily: "You describe a crime with a very soft tongue. I will ask the question more pointedly. Asrubal, where is the infant you kidnapped — which is to say, the son of Dain Maihac?"

Asrubal returned him a blank stare, then said: "I don't know."

"You don't know? How can this be?"

Asrubal shrugged. "At the time, and I freely admit this now, I was in a bad temper. I transferred the infant to my servants, with extremely brusque orders: remove the infant, keep him safe but out of my way. That is all I know."

The room was still. Tansett asked in a gentle voice: "Surely the information is at your disposition?"

"Yes, so I would suppose." Asrubal considered, then, turning, he signaled his chief steward. The two spoke together in quiet voices; then the steward hurried away.

Asrubal gave a quick nod of satisfaction. "The mystery shall soon be resolved. As it unfolds, it might well lay bare a fine irony, which you especially —" he indicated Jaro "— would appreciate."

Jaro stared at him uncomprehendingly.

Asrubal's steward entered the room. As before the two conferred; Asrubal gave a terse order. The steward hesitated the tenth part of a second, then bowed and departed.

Asrubal turned back to Tansett. "Now, as to my little conundrum: it is not so difficult, after all. Look yonder! There sits the son of Dain Maihac and a flighty woman of Sadaj House. He is young and handsome; he is the darling of Fortune!" He paused, but Jaro had nothing to say. Asrubal continued. "Long ago, I gave over the surety I had wrested from Dain Maihac to my servants. My mood was dark; I felt disheartened and angry; an out-worlder had come here to cheat me, to pilfer my goods, meanwhile grovelling and wheedling and crying out 'Virtue is mine!' How could I deal with this sly rodent? I maintained full estaing. I merely took surety, as is the time-honoured custom, and thus maintained the dignity of myself and Hoy House! I am a straightforward man! I deviate never from the course! I ordered the infant secured but kept from my sight and never to be referred to my notice until equipoise was satisfied. My orders were followed to the letter. The infant was taken deep, deep and deeper, to a hidden chamber down in the dark, and who can we blame for this fact? Who else but Dain Maihac, the faithless father who never returned to claim the surety? There is the answer; I have supplied you the proof! For fifteen years the person has been forgotten — until five minutes ago when I sent my steward to make inquiries." Asrubal pointed to the floor with a long white forefinger. "The chamber lies directly below where now we sit." Asrubal looked at Maihac. "Is this not the most delicious of ironies that you, the guilty man, sit in pomp above the dark dungeon where your son has sat in the dark?"

Maihac quivered, then could restrain himself no longer. He sprang across the chamber and struck out. Asrubal smilingly drew back and Maihac's fist drove though empty air. There became a turmoil of shouting, seething, snarling, panting shapes. Maihac was restrained but broke free, then once more was seized and borne to the floor. Asrubal mincingly stepped forward and deftly kicked Maihac in the face; then he too was brought under restraint.

After a time order was restored. Rufiel of Zank House spoke to Asrubal: "Am I to understand that you immured a child in a dungeon and held him there for fifteen years?"

"In the baldest of terms, this might be asserted. The fault of course lies elsewhere."

"Please answer the question in simple terms."

"Yes. I forgot his existence."

"He is now dead? Or alive?"

Asrubal shrugged. "My steward has gone to make a finding. When he returns, we shall hear the full particulars."

Silence held the chamber. Then Rufiel of Zank House said in a mild voice: "I suggest that the steward has been instructed to kill this unfortunate creature and hide the cadaver."

Asrubal turned a glacial stare upon Rufiel. "You have gone too far. Every cavalier of Hoy House will demand your blood. You will not survive the week."

Tansett spoke briefly to the elders of Hoy House, then said: "We have come to a consensus. Hoy House repudiates this individual. Asrubal speaks henceforth only on his own behalf. So far as we are concerned the Justiciars may issue their findings and their verdict."

Tansett said: "The Justiciars are agreed. We have carefully evaluated the complaint of Jaro and Dain Maihac against Asrubal. Jaro Maihac —" Tansett paused and looked around the chamber. "Jaro Maihac? Where are you? Jaro Maihac?"

Chapter 9

1.

Jaro watched as Asrubal gave instructions to the steward. He noticed the steward's hesitation and the hint of reluctance in his manner as he turned away to do Asrubal's bidding. Jaro, impelled by a sudden quiver of intuition, slid unobtrusively around behind the rear of the chamber and followed the steward: along a short passage, into a central hall.

Jaro halted, looked right and left. The steward was nowhere to be seen. Jaro feared that he had lost the trail. Then he noticed the last shudder of a heavy door as it settled into its jamb; Jaro ran across the hall, opened the door a slit looked to see a flight of descending steps. He listened and heard the shuffle of the steward's steps. Jaro followed: down, down, down. The air became clammy and dank; wan light issued from luminous wall-plaques. The steward's steps seemed to lose themselves; Jaro ran down the steps, as fast as he dared.

The stairs ended suddenly; Jaro jerked to a halt. Cautiously he peered into a room where a jailer sat at a table: like the steward, a high-caste servant.

The steward spoke, in a wry uncomfortable voice. Standing in the shadows of the passage, Jaro strained to hear. "I am here by order of the master. He believes that the creature you guard is still alive."

The jailer responded in a voice harsh and low: "He lives. This was the charge placed upon me."

"The master commands that he be killed at once, that the corpse be dropped into the deep hole, that the cell be cleaned and purged of the creature's presence. Haste is the tone of the command."

The jailer rose to his feet. He wore a black vest, short black leather breeches. "This makes for poor hearing."

"No matter; the master has uttered the order."

"Then it must be done." The jailer rose to his feet. "I will enter the cell with a light. He will turn his head away from the glare and I will strike him over the head with this iron stone-scraper. Then we will truss him into a blanket, drag him to the deep hole and in a trice the business is done. This is the easiest way, and there will be no filth to clean."

The jailer went to a door, slid back a shutter, his eye to the peep-hole. "He is inanimate; now is the time."

Jaro stepped out into the light. "The orders are countermanded."

"That cannot be," said the steward. "Asrubal of Hoy is our master; we must obey his orders."

"Open the door," said Jaro. "Bring out the prisoner and we will take him up to council hall. These are the new orders. You must obey. "

The jailer hurled the iron stone-scraper at Jaro; the steward held up a stool on high, and made as if to strike. Jaro killed them both with his gun.

The room was again silent. Jaro went to the door, put his eye to the peep-hole and thought to see the prisoner stir. He found a light switch, and brought light to the cell, then threw back the clamps on the door and eased it open. On a ragged mattress in the far corner lay a gaunt figure.

Jaro entered the cell; the prisoner raised to an elbow and blinked at Jaro. Jaro saw lank black hair, a straggling black beard, a face which was a pallid parody of his own.

Jaro found his voice. "Come; you are free; we are leaving this terrible place. Can you walk?"

Garlet said in a dreary voice: "Finally you have come."

"Yes, finally — as fast as I could."

Garlet heaved himself to a sitting position. He hunched and drew up his legs. "It was not fast enough."

"I know," said Jaro bleakly. "But I could do no better."

Garlet slowly rose to his feet. He studied Jaro suspiciously, head lowered to avoid the light. Jaro spoke soothingly: "Come; we'll go up the stairs. You are free of this dark prison."

Garlet swayed, as if he were ill, or intoxicated. He studied Jaro, blinking, as if he could not grasp the significance of Jaro's words.

Jaro spoke persuasively: "You don't know me but you can trust me." He held out his hand and stepped forward. The act triggered a reflex in Garlet's mind. He gave a choking, rasping cry and launched himself upon Jaro. Astonished, Jaro was driven back against the wall. Garlet's hair was thrust against his nose and mouth so that he could not breathe; then he struggled and, gasping, thrust the rancid body aside. He cried out: "Garlet! Don't fight me! I am Jaro, your brother!"

Garlet drew back, mouth convulsing. "I know you well enough! You are my evil skipping twin! You have lived the life of a prince; dancing and basking and sucking sweet juices while I paid the price, moaning here in the dark!"

"None of this is my fault!" cried Jaro.

Garlet grasped Jaro's shoulders with hands like steel clamps. "The years have passed; they are gone — all my days and my golden hours! You cannot pay the debt! What a tragedy! All that is precious and mine is gone! Now I do not care what happens!"

"That will change," said Jaro. "From now on —"

Garlet paid no heed. "First, I will kill you, and shall watch your blood flow into the drain."

Jaro gasped a protest. "That is not reasonable!"

"Who are you to say? I gave you your chance; I called to you, in a most pitiful way! But your only concern was to muffle my voice, lest it trouble your pleasure."

Jaro struggled and managed to escape Garlet's grip. He said, panting: "We can talk about this later, but let us leave this place now."

For response Garlet lunged forward and seized Jaro's throat. They toppled into a writhing heap; Garlet began to pound Jaro's head against the stone. "I will tear your eyes out," panted Garlet. "I shall lock you into the cell, then I will sit outside and be the jailer. I have long envied that man! Now I too can sit at my ease, free to walk either this way or that, to turn on or off the light as the mood strikes me; at every meal I shall eat salt fish with my gruel, and no one shall deny me vinegar!"

Jaro could not cope with the crazed strength of Garlet's arms; his senses slipped away from him, and he barely noticed the surge of shapes into the chamber. Garlet's weight was lifted away; he could breathe once more.

2.

After his initial paroxysms of emotion, Garlet had become drained and apathetic, though he watched everything and everyone with wary attention. He allowed himself to be washed, barbered, dressed in clean new clothes; then, somewhat sullenly, he joined the group which awaited him in a small drawing room at Sadaj House.

Garlet halted in the doorway, looking from face to face, then drew back a step and tried to turn away, or so it seemed. Then, responding to Abel Sadaj's hand on his arm, went to a couch at the side of the room and settled gingerly into the cushions. He peered distrustfully around at the gathering, which included Jaro, Skirl, where his gaze lingered, then to Dain Maihac and other members of the Sadaj household.

Garlet was treated with exaggerated punctilio. He was asked gentle questions, to which he responded in muffled monosyllables. Presently, in an adjoining refectory the group was served a light supper.

It was an uncomfortable meal. Garlet sat staring at the table, showing no disposition either to eat or to talk. Skirl prompted him: "Garlet, you must blank out the past and immerse yourself in the present and your future."

Garlet made no response, but his silence had a sardonic quality.

Skirl went on: "The past — it has slipped away; it is a whisper of a bad dream, no more! The future: with Jaro for a brother, it cannot help but be full of wonderful adventures!"

Garlet glanced at her sidelong. "Where will you be?"

Skirl smiled and shrugged. "I can't so much as guess."

"I want you to stay with me."

Skirl's smile became uncomfortable. "Have you tasted this wine? Just a sip; more might go to your head."

Garlet took note of the goblet, but made no move to touch it.

Dain Maihac, across the table, said: "If this is confusing, don't worry; it could hardly be anything else. So relax, and we'll make things as easy as possible for you."

Without raising his eyes from the goblet, Garlet said evenly: "I am not confused."

Maihac nodded slowly. "So much the better. Is there anything you want to know?"

"Not just now."

Skirl asked brightly: "Don't you want to talk? I should think that everything would seem wonderful, even exciting."

"There is too much to talk about."

Skirl thought to encourage him. "You must relax and say anything you like! We are all your friends. Jaro is your brother. Dain Maihac is your father."

"So it may be." Garlet spared each of the men a brief glance, then lowered his eyes to the goblet of wine. Skirl, looking from Jaro to Garlet, saw near-identity of feature, hairline and coloring. They were about of equal size, though Garlet was rather more lean than Jaro. There were subtle differences of posture, expression and mannerism. Skirl thought it odd that they resembled each other as much as they did, when the premises which defined their being were so different. She gently laid her fingers on his forearm. "Garlet, you must eat! Taste this tart! It is pastry filled with all good things."

"I do not care to eat now."

Skirl was puzzled. She leaned a little forward and looked into Garlet's face. "Why not? All the rest of us are eating."

Garlet's eyes narrowed. "Is it not clear? If I eat, I make myself part of the cabal."

Skirl shook her head. "Garlet, that is absurd! I am eating and I have joined no cabal. Far from it! I am Skirl Hutsenreiter, effectuator."

Garlet spoke indifferently: "Whatever you like."

Jaro, who had been watching Garlet, heard an overtone of bitterness which Garlet barely troubled to disguise. He said shortly: "I understand you well enough. In fact, I can't help but sympathize with you."

Garlet compressed his mouth, but made no response.

Dain Maihac spoke in a brisk voice. "Let us face facts. The doctors tell me that you cannot avoid psychological shock. For a time you will be under considerable stress and there is no predicting how you will deal with it. After a period of transition, you will feel easier with yourself and the world."

Garlet said evenly: "There is no need for concern. I feel neither shock nor distress."

Dain Maihac nodded. "Whatever the case, you need nourishment, and you should not starve yourself for irrational reasons."

"My reasons, whatever they are, seem rational to me. Still, you are right in one respect: I must transcend shadow-play." He reached out to a bowl of fruit, selected and ate a grape. "I will need strength for the task ahead." Without ceremony he rose to his feet and left the room. Skirl made an uncertain move, as if to go after him, but Jaro was first and Skirl settled slowly back into her chair.

Jaro followed Garlet out upon the terrace. Garlet went to lean on a balustrade and stood looking down into a pool where green and gold eels slid, aimless and languid, dreaming of destinations in their native Palmarene Sea. Above floated the two moons and Jaro was suddenly recalled to the image which had haunted him for years beyond his counting, of the twin moons shining into a garden such as this. He put the recollection from his mind. He asked Garlet, in a manner as gentle as he could contrive: "Why did you leave the table?"

Garlet darted Jaro a saturnine side-glance, but concluded that the question needed no answer.

Jaro spoke on, using a musing contemplative voice. "I will help you, in any way I can. In fact, we all will. But you must cooperate with us, and understand that for the moment you need us. So relax and be easy."

"I need no help."

"What of advice?"

"I need no advice."

Jaro laughed shortly. "You need both, very badly. You have a distorted view of the environment! It is pitiless! You must adapt yourself and your conduct to suit it, or in the end it will hurt you."

Garlet said softly: "I am my own environment, and I too am pitiless. I will do what needs to be done."

Jaro spoke in wonder: "What do you mean by that?"

"I have been caught up by a ponderous force. It is named necessity, and for which you are to blame. You came too late."

"I came as fast as I could!"

Garlet seemed not to hear. "I know little and I know much. From where I sat in the dark, I sent myself into your mind. You cared nothing; you betrayed me, and failed to listen, to heed, to feel. You hated me; you enjoyed your freedom while I huddled in the dark. I ate husks; you ate good things. Sometimes I thought to see glimpses of what you saw, and I tried to feel what you felt. I called to you; my cries were in vain. It is not fair. Either the white should be all white or the black all black."

Jaro puzzled a moment, then started to speak but Garlet made a curt gesture. "Do not say it. The force is irresistible." He looked closely at Jaro. "I suppose you think I am mad."

"Not altogether. I understand your mood quite well."

Garlet nodded. "Yes, no doubt. You are a clever one. I know this for a fact. Ah well, we shall see."

The two were joined by Skirl and Dain Maihac. After a moment Garlet allowed himself to be led to the chamber which had been set aside for his use. Standing beside a table of carved jade, he ate chunks of bread and cheese, then went to the far corner where he crept under a table and slept.

3.

Skirl set herself to the task of teaching Garlet the conventions and courtesies of ordinary life, though she could never be sure how deeply her lessons penetrated Garlet's opaque personality. Whatever the case, he clearly preferred her company to that of Jaro, no matter how assiduously Jaro attempted a friendly relationship.

Whatever Garlet's emotions, he gave none of them free expression. He remained taciturn and aloof, despite Jaro's best efforts at a constructive relationship. Garlet admitted that he knew nothing of reading and Jaro volunteered to teach him, but Garlet said that he was not yet ready to commit himself so far.

Meanwhile, at the Court of Justice, Asrubal had been adjudicated a criminal guilty of a dozen crimes. He was dishonoured, deprived of wealth and declared a pariah. Was he also guilty of murder? Here there was disagreement. One faction urged that Asrubal be executed — an opinion to which Asrubal, among others, could not concur. This second group argued that the death of Jamile Maihac had been an accident beyond Asrubal's control. They pointed out that he had no reason to kill her. They stated that guilt for the murder of Jamile was circumstantial and subject to a variety of explanations, since the deed occurred off-world, in a milieu notoriously coarse and wild. Jamile, by venturing into such an environment, had only herself to blame.

So went the thinking of certain Hoy elders. Their opponents laughed these contentions aside, and declared that Asrubal was clearly guilty, that he must be executed for the sake of equipoise. In the end the session was adjourned for five days at which time it was hoped that the factions might have reconciled their differences.

Dain Maihac, recalling that the previous legal episode had persisted over two years, was not pleased by the delay. He felt instinctively that the environment was not conducive to Garlet's mental health — what there was left of it.

Garlet's moods were inscrutable. He confided none of his thoughts or emotions to anyone, much less Dain Maihac, whom he seemed particularly to dislike and distrust. He relaxed only with Skirl. She, in turn, found him an interesting case-study, so to speak, and took it on herself to teach him basic social graces. In this enterprise she met only fair success, since Garlet's attention-span was brief. "You must apply yourself to these techniques," Skirl told him. "You will soon learn courtesy, gentility and, as a result, social acceptance."

"It is hardly worth the effort," muttered Garlet. "Teach me, by preference, the techniques of sex-play."

Skirl said at last: "These are ways and manners which lovers learn from each other, and so, in every case, are different. In any event, I am not an expert and I could only give you bad counsel."

Garlet made no comment and Skirl changed the subject.

Garlet was a difficult subject: so much became clear to Skirl. He lacked interest in the world Maz, the Gaean Reach, the cosmos. Skirl spoke to him of her life at Thanet and of Old Earth, which she had once visited on an excursion with her mother. Garlet listened passively but asked no questions. Skirl discovered that Garlet was unable to read and set herself to the task of teaching him., Garlet showed no initial interest in the program, but presently, after much encouragement from Skirl, applied himself to the task.

Jaro associated with Garlet as cautiously and diplomatically as possible. Garlet ignored him, to an almost insulting degree. When Dain Maihac appeared, Garlet became stiff and wary.

On the whole, Jaro was relieved that Garlet preferred Skirl's company to his own. One significant fact brought him great satisfaction: the voice at the back of his mind had vanished utterly, with such finality that Jaro knew it could never return.

Asrubal, subjected to house arrest, remained at the palace of his cousin Minto. Pleading 'mental fever', he secured an eight-day continuance to his trial. Dain Maihac, recalling his previous dealings with Roum law, was not surprised.

Jaro asked gloomily: "Does that mean another two- or three-year wait?"

"Definitely not," said Maihac. "On this occasion we control the momentum, not Asrubal. His only recourse is to kill us — so beware of duels, and accept no challenges."

Maihac and Jaro, sometimes with Skirl and occasionally with Garlet, wandered the old city, exploring abandoned palaces old beyond reckoning, their furnishings sound and as graceful as ever, save for the incremental dust. Once or twice they heard soft footsteps, though when they looked they saw nothing.

"House-ghouls," said Maihac. "They'll back away from us and keep to the shadows — unless we happen to separate."

Skirl glanced nervously to the back of the grand hall. "Then what?"

"Nothing nice. Don't worry about them now; they won't bother us. Come; look into here. This is the library."

Four shelves had at one time held two or three hundred volumes, most of which had now decayed into heaps of fiber and dust. Others, however, were sound and fresh as on the day they had been placed on the shelves. Jaro opened one of these books, whose dimensions were about fourteen inches high, ten inches wide and two inches thick. The pages, of thin pale-grey material, flexible but dense, were illuminated with a succession of beautiful drawings in colored inks: landscapes, interiors, portraits of a person engaged in various activities, all wrought with the most precise and felicitous technique Jaro had yet encountered. The colors, where employed, were vivid and appropriate: blues, scarlets, greens and purples and even more complicated compound colors. Jaro turned to Maihac for an explanation. "This book is amazing! Are they all like this?"

"More or less. The leaves are oxides and carbides of a dozen noble metals, powdered, deposited in a layer, flash-heated and compressed to a wafer-thin sinter. The material is imported, of course; there is no such technology on Maz. The pigments are permanent, also supplied by an off-world source. Once at Romarth, the book is then fashioned by hand. It represents a memorial to the person who created it. He worked all his life on this one book. It is his statement, the repository of all his secrets and all his private dreams. No one has examined it before, since such books are considered private. Still, here it is: someone's brave declaration that he was born, that he lived his life and that he experienced noble emotions which were worthy of record — even though no one might ever know them. Until now. You have looked into the book, and you are the first to do so, since the person who made the book closed the cover and clamped the seal for the last time."

Maihac turned pages in the book. "Here is his self-portrait, in a favorite costume. As you see, he was a handsome young man, dark-haired, somber, proud, defiant of destiny. The book is about two thousand years old. It is well wrought, but not a masterwork."

Jaro asked: "What of now? Do folk still create such books?"

"It's still being done; nothing ever changes at Romarth — but don't ask anyone about his book. It's considered bad form."

Jaro looked along the shelves. "There aren't many here; a hundred or so."

"Correct. They have no reverence for the old books. As soon as a man or a woman is safely forgotten, his book is consigned to a shelf in the Old Chemical Warehouse, and there they wait for the end of time."

Jaro said thoughtfully: "That is a sorry fate for such books. They deserve appreciation. If nothing else, they are valuable."

Dain Maihac nodded, showing the trace of a smile. "The thought has also occurred to me."

Jaro selected two books at random from the shelves and took them back to his chambers. Later in the day he studied them at length.

The first had been created two thousand years before by a gentleman attached to the now extinct House of Methune. His name was Latie and during the course of his life, using skills ever more expert, he depicted himself active in many capacities. Latie seemed a person of vivid imagination and a whimsical, occasionally astringent, personality, with an initial shyness which gradually dissolved as he matured into a person of quick intelligence if somewhat frail physique. At the age of ten he used a charming and naive style to depict himself as a nature sprite, clad in a kirtle of flowers with more flowers plaited into his hair. To the drawing were appended several verses the young Latie had composed and wished to perpetuate. Another drawing showed him as a youth, in company with a pretty girl of his own age. Both wore rather bizarre mummers' costumes, and apparently danced an intricate movement of some sort. Latie's skills were now well-developed; one drawing caught Jaro's attention and he studied it for several minutes. Depicted was Latie as a young cavalier, endowed with a slender, almost frail physique. Tendrils of waving brown hair framed his thin face. His large eyes were limpid gray-blue and looked directly from the drawing at Jaro; his delicate features well-shaped. The book contained very little text, but Latie had conjoined to the drawing a page inscribed with a declaration, or a fiat, addressed, so it would seem, to some anonymous all-encompassing intelligence, since Latie could never have foreseen that human eyes might explore his book. He wrote:

"So here am I, Latie of Methune: the one, the singularity, who is I. My qualities are excellent; they encompass virtue, humour, bliss, and honour. Need I say that there has never been another like me, and never shall the cosmos know my like again, since I stand at the apex of sentient life. How then have I transcended all others, across all of time? Have I performed prodigies? Have I solved the grand mysteries? How then? By my secret; why should I not yield truth? And this noble secret? It is tantalizing in its simplicity: it is my joy in being.

"So all you who come after: if you be beautiful maidens, sigh for a heartsick moment; if you be gallant cavaliers, shrug a regretful shrug; alas! None of you may conjoin the marching meter of my gorgeous life."

Jaro slowly laid aside the book of Latie, and took up the other. It had been created by a lady, Susumi of Meroe House. For much of her life she had enjoyed physical beauty, which she celebrated with artless abandon, and why not? since no one would ever learn of her indiscretions and escapades. Some of drawings fascinated Jaro: in one of these Susumi sat on the ledge of an arched window overlooking the river. She leaned back against one side, clasping one of her knees and looking out over the water. Trees shaded the palace and were reflected in the water; the scene was partly in sunlight and partly in shade, and conveyed a melancholy emotion. Looking closely, Jaro noticed the hint of detail in the shadows of the room behind her; as he studied the picture Jaro saw that a house-ghoul stood at the back of the room. The picture was intriguing in large part because of its ambiguity. Why the house-ghoul? Why the girl's lack of concern? Was she aware of the creature's presence? There was no explanation.

At breakfast on the following day Skirl was moved to inquire of Maihac in regard to the servants. "I can't understand them. They occupy distinctly inferior positions; they are treated without the slightest consideration for their feelings. They lack recreation, or self-expression, or any means of bettering themselves! Still they show no resentment; in fact, they seem quite resigned to their miserable existences. I can't help but feel indignant!"

"No need for that," said Maihac. "The servants are conditioned to take pleasure in service. It is a most interesting story, which I will explain if you are willing to listen."

Only Garlet indicated a lack of interest in the subject.

"The first settlers on Romarth were scientists; mostly biogeneticists, leaving behind an environment which seemed to them arbitrary and repressive, and which restricted the scope of their work. So they came to this splendid world Maz, where in utter isolation they might carry on such research as seemed consequential.

"From the first labor was a problem. They were intellectuals and had no taste for physical toil. They tried to hire a labor force, but the cost was exorbitant. So they decided to create their own ideal working class. They stipulated certain qualities; the typical servant must be agreeable, mild, gentle, devoid of an assertive sexuality. He was to be physically active, disease-resistant, well-coordinated, equipped with adequate intelligence, loyalty, a strong sense of responsibility. He was to be lean rather than burly, frugal in his diet, and versatile. His intellectual capacity must be sufficient that he might perform ordinary household and agricultural tasks, and physically attractive in the event that the servants might be required to perform sexual routines for their masters."

"Disgusting," muttered Skirl. "These men had the mentality of beasts."

Maihac shrugged. "They thought of themselves as 'intellectuals'. They designed a genetic manifold and set to work testing it and its variations. They made many adjustments. After predictable difficulties, they created the folk who are now the servants at Romarth. The structure now known as the Creche was built and the generative processors put into service. These processes still continue, since the servants were designed to be sterile, in order that, in the course of time, there might be no mutational drift away from the standard species.

"In general, the work was successful and the servants function as they were designed to do. When the servants become old, they are sent to a retirement village in the country, where they live out their days, and replacements are secured from the Creche; there are no atrocities, no cruelty.

"So far, so good. The factors of Old Romarth seem to have solved their problem with flair. But mistakes were also made, and in this connection a hundred rumors run wild.

"They center around a director of the project name Drip Liloc. For purposes now obscure he created a rogue species, capable of reproduction, with qualities maleficent rather than benevolent. Some say he was fascinated by a challenge to create a humanoid creature of absolutely evil characteristics, and irresponsibly he toyed with the concept. In the end, he produced beings which escaped from the Creche and which now infest the steppes: the Loclor.

"A hundred years later a geneticist named Voil Volhove — not really a nice man; I admit to this in advance — also attempted experiments. He seems to have attempted fornication with one of his productions. His motive, so he declared, was simple curiosity, or the impulse which causes men to scale high mountains; he did it, in short, because it was there! Skirl, did you speak?"

"I am skeptical."

"Yes, of course. In any event, the results were both grotesque and tragic. The creature spawned twins, male and female. Voil Volhove, fascinated, allowed the creatures to survive in a secret pen where they could do as they liked. They bred with great intensity of purpose. One day they killed Voil Volhove, wandered away into the forest and became the house-ghouls. That, so far as I can gather, is how these odd creatures originated.

"Since then thousands of years have gone by. The Loclor have taken control of Maz, except in the forests. The house-ghouls cannot be eradicated; the servants still originate in the Creche and are now essential to the Roum, who could not survive without them. Perhaps it is a form of symbiosis. The Roum produce few children; they are gradually waning in numbers and the future must seem uncertain."

"I would not care to be the last Roum in Romarth," said Jaro.

Maihac nodded. "Before that time, they will have moved back into the Reach. Money is their life; Asrubal's financial crimes horrify them more than murder. If you are interested, I will take you to the Creche; it is open to visitors, though it is not a place one cares to linger."

Jaro and Skirl agreed to the excursion. Jaro suggested to Garlet that he might wish to accompany them, but Garlet refused. Jaro tried to be easy and companionable. "Oh, come along! It will be good for you. You must stop your moping and start going about with me."

"I think not."

Jaro considered Garlet thoughtfully. Strange how, in some respects, the two resembled each other, but in others were as different as night from day! Strange indeed, when they had evolved from the same primal cell!

Jaro politely explained to Garlet that the excursion could not help but interest him, since it demonstrated the means by which servants were transformed from zygotes to infants in a succession of tubes, tubs and vats, then sorted, tested, placed in growth chambers and inculcated with those reflex responses which would be most useful in their special sort of work.

Garlet still demurred. He would rather go out to sit on the terrace which overlooked the boulevard, where he could watch the gallant cavaliers and the charming ladies of Romarth at their promenades.

At times they paused at tree-shaded cafés, to sip herbal infusions or chilled wine, but soon they would stroll on to a new destination. The cavaliers saluted each other with grave politesse, and meanwhile paid their respects to the maidens, in their many-colored garments. It was a splendid spectacle, which Jaro himself found pleasant. Garlet however had become fascinated with the parade of gallant cavaliers and lovely ladies. Given Garlet's apparent preference for isolation Jaro found his behaviour hard to understand.

Jaro saw that his arguments were futile. He said rather heavily: "Enjoy the parade while you can; there is nothing like it elsewhere, so soak it up. Before long we'll be gone."

Garlet turned him a suspicious glance, but made no comment. Jaro went off to join Maihac and Skirl.

Maihac led the way along the river embankment to the Creche, which was housed in a stark rectangular structure on the two lower floors, with warehouses above. From the boulevard an entry split into a pair of ramps: the first leading up to the Old Chemical Warehouse, the second descending to a complex of deserted offices. Beyond a balcony overlooked the main workroom from three sides. Signs warned visitors to keep to the balconies; to conduct themselves with discretion; to do nothing to disturb the work below, which was truly delicate and important. Very few Roum took advantage of the balcony to inspect the processes which provided them their all-important servants. In the first place there was little to see save a maze of tubes, generators, vats, tanks and steaming cauldrons. Among these articles of apparatus moved dozens of technicians, of a special self-perpetuating caste, who communicated almost never with the Roum. From the pots and vats of ambiguous substances rose an odor which in many instances brought nausea to the visitors. Maihac ignored the odor; Skirl and Jaro pretended indifference but none wasted time on the balcony, and the visit to the Creche took somewhat less time than Jaro had expected.

As they departed, he halted by the up-ramp, recalling an item of information imparted to him by Maihac. "Did you say that this is the Old Chemical warehouse, where all the ancient books are stored?"

"So I did."

Jaro said no more. Skirl might not approve of what he had in mind, and he did not care to argue that his actions harmed no one, while perhaps bringing joy and wonder to others, and almost certainly considerable money to themselves. Skirl would then have insisted that such money be transferred back to Maz and turned over to the Roum, and for this course of action Jaro would not be able to supply any cogent response, except to declare that he did not propose to follow this highly moral course of action.

On the following day, late in the afternoon, while walking in the street, Jaro was jostled by a young bravo of Hoy House and challenged to a duel.

Jaro declined the offer, which enraged Cong Hoy. He took his hat and slapped Jaro across the face with it. Jaro seized the hat and threw into the river. "That is a mortal insult," cried Cong Hoy, and snatched out his sword. "I have every right to pierce you through and through, and I shall surely do so."

The cavalier waved his sword over his head in a flourish of great virtuosity. Jaro stepped forward and wrested the sword from Cong's grasp and threw it into the river as well. Then he struck Cong with his fist. Cong staggered back in confusion. Jaro frog-marched him to the balustrade and heaved him over into the slime beside the river.

"That is amusing," said certain cavaliers who had stopped to watch. "Still it is not the proper mode in which to conduct a duel."

"Wrong!" Jaro told them. "I was refusing to conduct a duel. That is the source of your mistake."

"Ah! It is still an unconventional sequence of tactics."

"Still, I have made myself clear, and he'll think twice before he challenges me again."

"Tut tut!" said one of the cavaliers. "To avoid duels is the way of a coward and a scoundrel."

"Your poor opinion will cause me great pain," said Jaro politely.

4.

Skirl continued to teach Garlet the rudiments of reading, despite the waning of his interest. Nevertheless, he still preferred Skirl's company to that of Jaro. The reason for this partiality became clear when one day Garlet began to fondle her breasts. Skirl jumped back in surprise, thereby arousing Garlet's displeasure. He was now erotically excited and approached Skirl, grinning in apparent invitation. Skirl danced and dodged about the room, meanwhile explaining that Garlet's conduct was in very bad taste. She ordered Garlet to behave himself and to resume his lessons. At this moment Jaro appeared in the doorway, where he stood watching the two as they moved about the room. Skirl at last managed to take refuge beside him, where she stood breathing hard. "Garlet is being a bit forward," she told Jaro. "I don't feel that I care to teach him any longer."

Garlet looked from one to the other, then, with a set face, turned and stalked from the room.

Skirl said bleakly: "Now it's your turn; you must do what is necessary."

"I don't intend to teach him," said Jaro. "Once back in civilization we'll find him a tutor." He prepared to take his leave. Skirl asked anxiously, "Where are you going?"

"I'm going to take another look at the Creche. Do you want to come?"

Skirl wrinkled her nose and shook her head. "I can't abide the smell in the place. It's like burnt soup and some other stuff I don't like to think about."

"Agreed; it is a bad smell."

Jaro went alone to the Creche, but climbed the up-ramp into the Old Chemical warehouse. There he busied himself among the ancient books. Later, during the evening, he dropped the flitter upon a cargo dock, loaded aboard six cartons of books, carried them aloft to the *Pharsang*, unloaded them into the cargo bay, and returned to Romarth.

5.

During the morning of the following day, Asrubal demanded another continuance, which was granted, but during the evening a rare but not unprecedented event occurred. A group of cavaliers, all wearing masks of green mesh*, to signify themselves as Liltics, entered Hoy House

---

* The green mesh masks were not designed to conceal identity, but to represent

and seized Asrubal. They gagged him, stripped him to his undergarments, conveyed him by twilight to an ancient mansion in a far section of Old Romarth. They shackled his ankles to a tree, then, as night came to Romarth and the two moons rose to illuminate the garden the Liltics departed and their voices dwindled and could be heard no more.

From the house, moving silently, as if not wishing to be heard, came a shrouded shape, followed by another. For several moments they stood looking at Asrubal, who stared back, fascinated.

membership in the Liltics: an ancient secret society sworn to serve the cause of justice. Because of Liltic involvement, Asrubal's fate was far more harsh than might have been the case otherwise. It may be noted that the epithet hurled by the Liltics against the quivering Asrubal, was more often than not: "Peculator!". The crimes of murder, kidnap and immurement seemed of lesser consequence to the Liltics.

Chapter 10

1.

News of Asrubal's death swiftly became current. Maihac, Skirl and Jaro made plans to depart as soon as practicable. The Liltics agreed to transport a committee to Mibbs or elsewhere, that they might establish the fabric of a new commercial system. Maihac also recommended that armed expeditions be sent out to exterminate the Loclor but no one seemed to give the suggestion more than polite attention. The Roum contingent would be ready to depart in two days time. Maihac and Jaro conferred with Garlet, announcing the departure. He frowned as if he found the news disturbing. "I am not sure that I want to leave this place," he told them.

"This is no place for you," Maihac told him. "You would become a mental vegetable, like these other Roum. The race is decadent; it is obsessed by its intricate rituals. You do not know the rituals; you would be a fish out of water."

"Jaro knows these rituals well enough," said Garlet obstinately. "He can teach me; it is the least he can do."

"What?" cried Jaro. "In two days? Ridiculous!"

Maihac tried to speak reasonably. "There is nothing for you to do! You would become very unhappy."

Garlet said mulishly: "I am content to sit on the terrace and watch the Roum pass by at their promenades. Already I have seen several young women of haunting beauty, and I intend to become intimate with them."

"It is not so easy," said Maihac. "These young women may well be polite but I doubt if any will wish to become intimate with you. Like everyone else, these girls are constricted by convention, and the art of Roum love-making is elaborate indeed."

Garlet gave his head an angry shake. "Jaro will speak to them, and explain what their responses should be, in the special circumstances. I will trust him to make the arrangements."

Maihac smiled. "Jaro does not intend any sojourn here on Maz; he is as anxious to leave as I am."

Garlet, frowning in puzzlement, turned to Jaro. "If I stay, then you must stay, for compelling reasons."

"Not so," said Jaro. "I cannot get off this weird world fast enough. You will feel the same way, presently."

"That is hardly a gracious thing to say."

Jaro shrugged. "It is a fact which cannot be denied."

Garlet turned away and looked stonily off across the boulevard.

Later in the day Jaro slipped away from the palace and set off toward the Creche, intending to make another selection among the books of the Old Chemical Warehouse. He followed the embankment downstream to the ugly old structure; as he turned into the entryway, he looked over his shoulder and found to his surprise and annoyance that Garlet had followed him.

Jaro waited. Garlet approached and halted, showing a suspicious expression. He asked: "Where are you going?"

For a variety of reasons Jaro did not wish to reveal his true purposes to Garlet. "This is the Creche," he told Garlet. "It is an interesting place."

"I will come with you."

"As you like." Jaro would take Garlet along the balcony, where, so he suspected, Garlet would soon become bored with the steam and the stench. He started down the ramp. "Come along."

Garlet nodded pensively. Jaro wondered what was going on in his mind. Impossible to guess. Jaro led the way into the outer offices and out upon the balconies. As Jaro had expected, a perfunctory glance about was enough for Garlet. He told Jaro brusquely: "I have seen enough; the smell is bad. Let us leave."

"Go, if you like," said Jaro. "I intend to stay."

"No! Come away from here; this is not to my liking."

"Then go."

"No," said Garlet stubbornly. "I wish to talk with you. Come."

Jaro, restraining his annoyance followed Garlet into one of the near offices. "So — what do you wish to say?"

"I want you to understand me." Garlet's voice was superficially reasonable. "I have done much thinking and I now have grasped the broad pattern which unifies the universe. It is balance. Between us, this balance has been warped, so that now distortion is everywhere."

"That is only your point of view," said Jaro. "I have no such problem."

"Silence, if you please, while I am speaking. The distortion exists. It is a matter of identity. We stand here. Which is 'I' and which is 'he'? So far a certain 'Jaro' has proudly used the word 'I', while the miserable 'Garlet' was no more than a huddle in the dark with little use even for the word 'he', or a hint or a whisper. That is life at its most archaic! But I was receptive! You and I were the same stuff, and there was resonance between us. I became able to watch from the dark! I began to know yearning; it was like dawn arriving upon chaos. As the years passed I discovered a special quality; I name it 'iaa'. It may have meaning for you, but no one else will understand. Does the word carry meaning to your mind?"

"No."

"Hmm. It is because I devised the sound myself, and so, I fear it is a bit arbitrary. The word has a special but universal meaning: that is to say, the exercise of free will and choice among many pleasant choices. To put it another way, 'iaa' means the use of free will in a mood of glory and elation. The idea sustained me during early times. Sitting in the dark, I might hold a finger close to my face, and here was the 'iaa': should I touch my nose or my chin? I did not know; the future was veiled; the denouement was secret! I might sit for minutes on end waiting for the iaa to resolve, and here was drama indeed! And then, without forethought the finger moved. A thrilling moment! Marvellous to state, the finger might touch neither nose nor chin, but go to an ear, as if impelled by a mischievous imp! Here was iaa in its purest essence! It began to elude me when I sensed your life and its many little gluttonies. My calls only made you hug your privileges more tightly. Now there is change. Destiny has altered its face and swings back on its course; it is an era of adjustment. We will stay at Romarth. 'Garlet' shall be the 'I' and 'Jaro' the 'he', and his dismay must be subdued by stoicism. This implies that there will be variations in our joy. In this regard, we must engage the sympathy and the interest of the lovely maidens who saunter the streets in such a tempting profusion. Have you any program in this connection?"

"Of course not. I am leaving Romarth as soon as possible."

"No," said Garlet with decision. "You will stay here with me. Why? Because equipoise implies redress! I am entitled to solace! If necessary, and to this end you might well wish to do a stint in the dungeons to show the sincerity of your grief."

Jaro listened in awe and astonishment. Garlet was not necessarily mad; by the tenets of his own universe he might be wise, but in the new environment the mental tools he had fashioned so painfully were useless.

Jaro spoke gently. "Garlet, believe this as fact: I had no part in your misfortunes and I will accept no guilt. I will help you to a reasonable extent — but, once and for all, I am not staying with you at Romarth. I want you to come away, perhaps to Gallingale, and start a new life."

Garlet said nothing. Jaro started back toward the balcony. Instead of returning the way he had come, Garlet followed him out upon the balcony. The stench of steaming organic pastes and slurries rose to envelope him. Behind Jaro, Garlet made a sound of disgust. "Come away from here."

Jaro went to lean on the balcony, as if absorbed in the wonderful processes taking place fifty feet below. He thought that Garlet had turned away, returning to the outer offices, but he feigned indifference. Then he felt the vibration of footsteps, slow, ponderous, fateful. He turned to look over his shoulder. Garlet had secured a metal bar from the office; he was now striking down at Jaro's head. Jaro cringed, ducked, and took the blow glancingly on the muscular pad at the back of his shoulder. It staggered him and sent him sprawling. Garlet stood over him, club raised for a more accurate blow. Jaro frantically twisted aside, pulled out his gun; the bar struck his arm and the gun fell to the floor. Jaro scrambled on hands and knees for the gun; Garlet kicked him and took up the gun. He pointed it at Jaro. Slowly, painfully, Jaro rose to his feet.

Garlet spoke. "This is the ultimate iaa. Shall I kill you at the count of five or at the count of ten? Or perhaps twenty? Shall I blow away your legs — or your head? The indecision is a delight; it is iaa. I shall not know what is ultimately done until I do it."

"Garlet! Be reasonable! Put the gun down!"

"Notice my patience," said Garlet boastfully. "The tension swells; it is about to bubble, to burst!"

"Garlet! I am your brother! I can help you!"

Garlet smiled. "Nothing prevails. I have been hurt beyond any hope of redemption. Now — iaa closes my finger! I shoot."

Garlet had not released the safety; as he fumbled with the toggle; Jaro dropped flat. Releasing the safety, Garlet moved the toggle to 'Maximum', fired the gun; the bolt passed over Jaro and slanted down to strike an energy accumulator, causing an explosion of blue flame. Garlet fired again, and again. Jaro rolled aside; the bolts struck a retort, which burst, smashing a complex mesh of glass tubes. Jaro, on hands and knees, scuttled for protection. Garlet circled about, hoping for a clear shot. He aimed, fired; the charge passed wide of Jaro, struck into the great glass globe of mother-substance, which split and broke, spilling the base plasma down upon the accumulator, which exploded, and the interior of the Creche was a tangle of shards and twisted metal and screaming technicians. Garlet blinked, gaped in wonder at the devastation below. Jaro sprang at Garlet, wrested away the gun, swung around to face his brother.

For a moment the two stood in silence, glaring at each other. Then Garlet softly crept forward. Jaro raised the gun, but could not shoot his brother. He backed away, but Garlet rushed at him; the two clinched. Garlet was astonishingly strong; he flung Jaro to the floor; then picked him up that he might toss Jaro over the balcony. Jaro caught Garlet's head, twisted it to the side: far, far, grotesquely askew. Garlet cried out, dropped Jaro. Panting, Jaro rose to his feet. Garlet staggered toward him; Jaro struck him on the jaw with all his force; Garlet reeled backward to the balustrade, toppled over backward, and fell into a cauldron, which broke, to destroy a bank of control apparatus. Jaro forced himself to look down. What he saw caused his viscera to twist in disgust and horror and pity. He left and ran from the Creche at best speed.

2.

Jaro returned at best speed to (Coralie) Sadaj Palace. He reported events to Dain Maihac; they instantly found Skirl and boarding the flitters departed Romarth for the *Pharsang*. Below them the Folle Vanitia became crowded with the stunned folk of the city, who only gradually understood that there would be no new servants. Who would perform the toil which allowed them to live their pleasant lives? Who would till the soil and provide them sustenance? They asked the questions of one another, but none had answers. Could it be that the era of life at Old Romarth had come to an end? They could either perform the toil with their own hands or they could emigrate to the barbarian worlds of the Gaean Reach and establish new existences for themselves. If they did nothing, they would fall victim to the house-ghouls, who would inherit Romarth.

Gradually it became known that the off-worlders had caused the disaster. A great fury overtook the folk of Romarth; had Jaro or Maihac or Skirl been on hand, they would have fared badly. But the *Pharsang* was already far distant, fleeting back toward Yellow Rose Star and the world Gadron.

3.

At Mibbs Maihac and Jaro decided to become traders and operators of a transport service among the remote and out-of-the-way worlds of the Reach, where more often than not no scheduled services were available. It was a vagabond career, for someone anxious to live a life of adventure, color, pageantry, customs strange and wonderful. There would also be vicissitudes, uncertainties, occasionally danger if only the risk of a brawl in some remote saloon. Skirl decided that it was not a life she cared to lead, especially since she would be in close proximity with Dain Maihac. Her feeling toward Maihac was not so much dislike as distrust, uneasiness and inadequacy. He was a man she could never be able to persuade, or wheedle, or command, or charm, or persuade by any of the methods with which she was familiar. Jaro was more malleable. She thought she could take Jaro in hand and make of him the proud intelligent socially admired person who might even be voted into the Society of Clam Muffins, if all went well. Jaro however, was inseparable from his father, so that must be the way of it. When Skirl announced her decision to return to Thanet and set up shop as an effectuator, neither Maihac nor Jaro seemed surprised, nor did they urge her to change her mind, which rather nettled her. However, they pressed upon her two hundred thousand sols, which after a few moments of hesitation she accepted with thanks. She was, after all leaving them with six hundred thousand sols and more, along with the *Pharsang*.

Skirl departed for Gallingale aboard a passenger packet. As they watched the ship rise into the sky, Jaro said pensively: "At one time I thought that I was in love with Skirl. But I never dared do anything about it."

Dain Maihac laughed. "She is very pretty; she is also very strong-minded, and a Clam Muffin as well."

"Yes. That is true."

Jack Vance was born in 1916 to a well-off California family that, as his childhood ended, fell upon hard times. As a young man he worked at a series of unsatisfying jobs before studying mining engineering, physics, journalism and English at the University of California Berkeley. Leaving school as America was going to war, he found a place as an ordinary seaman in the merchant marine. Later he worked as a rigger, surveyor, ceramicist, and carpenter before his steady production of sf, mystery novels, and short stories established him as a full-time writer.

His output over more than sixty years was prodigious and won him three Hugo Awards, a Nebula Award, a World Fantasy Award for lifetime achievement, as well as an Edgar from the Mystery Writers of America. The Science Fiction and Fantasy Writers of America named him a grandmaster and he was inducted into the Science Fiction Hall of Fame.

His works crossed genre boundaries, from dark fantasies (including the highly influential *Dying Earth* cycle of novels) to interstellar space operas, from heroic fantasy (the *Lyonesse* trilogy) to murder mysteries featuring a sheriff (the Joe Bain novels) in a rural California county. A Vance story often centered on a competent male protagonist thrust into a dangerous, evolving situation on a planet where adventure was his daily fare, or featured a young person setting out on a perilous odyssey over difficult terrain populated by entrenched, scheming enemies.

Late in his life, a world-spanning assemblage of Vance aficionados came together to return his works to their original form, restoring material cut by editors whose chief preoccupation was the page count of a pulp magazine. The result was the complete and authoritative *Vance Integral Edition* in 44 hardcover volumes. Spatterlight Press is now publishing the VIE texts as ebooks, and as print-on-demand paperbacks.

Colophon

This book was printed using Adobe Arno Pro.
Book Composition and Typesetting: Joel Anderson
Art Direction and Cover Design: Howard Kistler
Proofing: David A. Kennedy, Dave Worden
Jacket Blurb: Steve Sherman, John Vance
Management: John Vance, Koen Vyverman